KEEP GOING – KEEP GROWING
The onward journey of the steward

KEEP GOING – KEEP GROWING
The onward journey of the steward

by

G. H. & E. F. Grose

Published for

CNI Stewardship Committee

by

ISPCK, Delhi
1998

Keep Going–Keep Growing (The onward journey of the steward):
Published by Rev. Ashish Amos for the Indian Society for Pro-
moting Christian Knowledge, Post Box 1585, Kashmere Gate,
Delhi–110006 for the Stewardship Committee of the Church of
North India; CNI Bhawan, 16 Pandit Pant Marg, New Delhi-
110001

First Published 1996

Reprinted 1998

ISBN: 81-7214-302-7

Laser typeset and cover design by
ISPCK, Post Box 1585, 1654, Madarsa Road,
Kashmere Gate, Delhi–110006, Phone: 2966323,
Fax: 91-11-2965490, *Grams:* LITHOUSE
E-mail: ispck@nde.vsnl.net.in
Internet: www.acpl.com/ISPCK

Contents

FOREWORD

Economic liberalisation and electronic media explosion have brought an unexpected threat to the Indian society and the Indian Church in particular. Many questions have risen, specially in the minds of the youth, about the need and validity of the ethos and values which have held our culture, society and the Church together.

Modernisation and scientific applications are welcome developments. But they have their brighter as well as darker sides. We needed an appropriate fence from their ills. This is where the Indian Church felt a vacuum. We needed to protect the hearts and minds of our younger generation before the seeds of life controlling problems were sown into them.

'Keep going, keep growing' is a befitting response to the need of the hour. The book is realistically simple, practically Christian and essentially biblical. Who could have contributed to this need of the Indian Church better than Rev. & Mrs. Grose? They know the Western culture and the Indian mind. 'Keep going, keep growing' is enriched with their many years of pastoral and teaching experience. I'm sure that the Indian Church would find the book to be a light house in the troubled waters of changing values and ethos.

The Rt. Rev. L. R. Tandy,
Bishop, Sambalpur Diocese,
President Stewardship Committee.

PROLOGUE

An Introduction to the
Church of North India

(a) History*

The Church of North India is a united church which came into being as the result of a union of six churches on 29th November 1970. The six churches were:

(1) The Council of the Baptist Churches in Northern India.

(2) The Church of the Brethren in India.

(3) The Disciples of Christ.

(4) The Church of India (also formerly known as the Church of India, Pakistan, Burma and Ceylon).

(5) The Methodist Church (British and Australasian Conferences).

(6) The United Church of Northern India.

These churches were all linked with the church of the apostolic times by an essential continuity of doctrine, of experience and of allegiance to the Lord Jesus Christ, and by a fellowship in the continued proclaiming of the message of salvation through Him. In different ways they had all sought to maintain continuity with the primitive church in matters of order.

Traces of the movement towards a re-union of Christian denominations (or churches) in India may be seen as far back as 1810 when William Carey called a conference of all Christian denominations at Cape Town for a mutual sharing of missionary experiences on common problems. But this movement becomes more visible in

---

* Taken from "The Joint Council of CNI, CSI & MTC" edited by J. Russel Chandran, ISPCK, 1984

the famous International Missionary Conference held in Edinburgh (Scotland) in 1910 which is commonly acclaimed as the origin of the twentieth century world-wide ecumenical movement. In India this movement began to take the concrete shape of "negotiations" for "organic unity", or "re-union" of churches from the famous Tranquebar Conference of 1919. This conference issued a challenging statement which included the following words:

> We believe that the challenge of the present hour calls us to mourn our past divisions and turn to our Lord Jesus Christ to seek in Him the unity of the body expressed in one visible Church. We face together the titanic task of the winning of India for Christ–one fifth of the human race. Yet confronted by such an overwhelming responsibility, we find ourselves rendered weak and relatively impotent by our unhappy divisions– divisions for which we were not responsible, and which have been, as it were, imposed upon us from without.*

One very significant and concrete result of the climate created by the Tranquebar Conference of 1919 was the union of the various Presbyterian and Congregational churches which took place in 1924, evolving "The United Church of Northern India". The first assembly of this church met in 1924. It sent out an invitation to other churches urging them to seek ways of expressing the Church's oneness in Christ. In this way the United Church of Northern India became pioneers in the Church Union movement in North India. Its constitution (which came to be known as the 'Blue Book') expresses this Church's desire "to work towards a wider union of churches" in India and Pakistan (Chapter VIII, Section 2 (iii)).

As the movement for Church Union gathered momentum, a Round Table Conference was called at Lal Bagh Girls' School, Lucknow, on 10th-11th April 1929, to consider the possibility of a re-union of churches. This turned out to be the first of a series of Round Table Conferences which, after the inauguration of the Church of South India on September 27, 1947, paved the way for the ap-

---

* Cited from *Forward to Union*, I.S.P.C.K. Delhi, and L.P.H. Lucknow, 1968, p. 2.

pointment of a Negotiating Committee for Church Union in North India. The first meeting of this Negotiating Committee was held at Calcutta in 1951. The proposed *Plan of Church Union in North India* was drawn up. This plan was further revised in 1954 and 1957. When it was presented to the negotiating churches for decision, they encountered certain difficulties in accepting it, and raised some questions. In the light of these the Negotiating Committee further revised the plan. It was this fourth edition of the *Plan of Church Union in North India and Pakistan*, published in 1965, which formed the basis for Church Union in North India. The Negotiating Committee commended this 4th edition of the plan (1965) to the negotiating churches for their decision and urged them to communicate their decision to the Secretary of the Negotiating Committee by March 1969. The negotiating churches took the proposed Plan of Church Union to their respective members at different levels for study and opinion, and subsequently considered it through their appropriate representative decision-making legislative and executive bodies. Six of the seven negotiating churches voted in favour of the plan and decided to enter into the Union.

(b) The Union

The Union of the six churches was inaugurated, as planned, on Sunday, November 29, 1970, at All Saints' Cathedral, Nagpur. This Service included the Declaration of Union and the Representative Act of the Unification of the Ministry. At this memorable Service the duly authorised lay representatives of the six uniting churches read out the declarations of their respective churches accepting the Plan of Church Union in North India (4th edition)- including Part I, the Constitution, and Part II, regarding the Inauguration of Union and Interim Arrangements, and solemnly placed these declarations, together with the declaration of the bishops and other ordained ministers accepting the Plan and the Consititution of the Church of North India, on the communion table. The presiding minister solemnly declared that "these six Churches within the area of union have become one CHURCH OF NORTH INDIA". The Representative Act of the Unification of the Ministry was subsequently carried over to the nineteen dioceses where through a Service of Unification of the Ministry, all the ordained ministers of the six churches which had united were unified into the ordained ministry of the Church of North India.

(c) The Six Churches which United

The Union of November 29, 1970 was a unique event in that six churches with diverse doctrinal positions, liturgical practices and polity or church–government united into one church–The Church of North India. The reaching of agreements on the many differences was not easy and was possible only because of the grace and guidance of the Holy Spirit. The diversity of traditions was not lost in the Union but it continues to contribute to the strength and richness of the Church of North India.

1. The Council of Baptist Churches in Northern India

The first Baptist churches emerged in Europe in the early 17th century. They professed that baptism could only be administered by immersion and to those who consciously profess their faith in Jesus Christ and also express their repentance of sins. The Baptist Missionary Society was founded on 2nd October, 1792, in England, and William Carey was its first missionary. He came to India in 1793. The several hundred congregations of Baptists which were members of the *Council of the Baptist Churches in Northern India*, mostly located in U.P., Delhi, Bihar, Orissa, Bengal, Assam and Nagaland, owed their origin to the work of the Baptist Missionary Society initiated by William Carey in Bengal. At the time of the Union the membership of the Baptist Churches which were represented in the Church Union negotiations by the *Council of the Baptist Churches in Northern India* was 1,10,000. These churches had a congregational form of church-government, each congregation being responsible for its own ministry and form of worship. They were strongly evangelical in faith and emphasised the need for personal holiness in life.

2. The Church of the Brethren in India

The Church of the Brethren originated in Germany and many of its members migrated to America in the 18th century, where it flourished. *The Brethren* have been deeply committed to peace- making and are opposed to war. *The Church of the Brethren in India* emerged as a result of the work begun in 1895 by missionaries from America.

At the time of the Union *The Church of the Brethren* had its congregations mainly in the States of Maharashtra and Gujarat. These were organised under the First District and the Second District of *The Church of the Brethren,* and had a membership of about 18,000. One important annual observance of this church, which with some modification has found a place in the growing liturgical tradition of the Church of North India, was a gathering for worship which included acts of peace-making, baptisms, preaching, mutual feet-washing and a Love Feast–a reenactment of the Last Supper which the Lord Jesus ate with his disciples on the night before his crucifixion.

3. The Disciples of Christ

This church originated in the U.S.A. in 1811 in protest against some of the doctrines and practices of the Calvinistic churches. It called the churches to unity and to the pattern of the church of the New Testament times, which included the practice of believers' baptism and the celebration of the Lord's Supper as the central act of worship. In India *The Disciples* missionaries started work in 1882, and established congregations in what is now Madhya Pradesh. The local congregations of *The Disciples* were autonomous and evangelical in faith and commitment. At the time of the Union their membership was about 16,000.

4. The Church of India

The Church of India (also formerly known as the Church of India, Pakistan, Burma and Ceylon, the CIPBC) was the only episcopal church, i.e. a church which had bishops in its ordained ministry of "bishops, priests and deacons handed down from the primitive church". It was a province of the Anglican communion having a relationship with the Church of England, but with complete autonomy since 1927. It grew out of the work of Anglican missionary societies–the Society for the Propagation of the Gospel, and the Church Missionary Society–which began their work early in the 19th century. At the time of the Union it had thirteen dioceses, each under a bishop, and it was governed by its General Council composed of all bishops and representatives of dioceses. The Bishop of Calcutta was also the Metropolitan of this church who presided

over the Episcopal Synod (a meeting of the bishops) and also over
the General Council. It had a distinct and rich liturgical tradition
and a Book of Common Prayer which contained its forms of worship and of celebration of the sacraments. Its membership was approximately 2,80,000.

5. The Methodist Church (British and Australian Conferences)

The origins of this church go back to the revival ministry of John
Wesley and Charles Wesley which began in England in the latter
part of the 18th century. It emphasised a personal commitment to
Jesus Christ, salvation through faith, holiness of life and fellowship
of believers. In India it grew out of the evangelistic work begun by
British and Australian missionaries of *The Methodist Church* in the
latter half of the 19th century. At the time of the Union it had two
districts (one in Bengal and the other in the Lucknow-Benares areas) with a membership of about 20,000. These were organised on
the Presbyterian system of church-government with a representative to annual conferences.

6. The United Church of Northern India

This church evolved out of a union of Presbyterian and Congregational churches in 1924. The congregations of the Congregational
and Presbyterian churches in North India were established by the
work of missionaries from Britain, the USA, Canada, Australia and
New Zealand.

   The doctrinal position of these missionaries was generally Calvinistic. They emphasised preaching and exposition of the Word of
God, moral discipline, unity of churches and Christian social action. *The United Church of Northern India* was organised according to the Presbyterian system of local congregations, church coun-
cils, synods and the General Assembly. It had also developed its
own liturgy and forms of worship which were published in a book
called *United Church Worship*. The membership of that part of this
church which came into the Union (i.e. excluding the North-Eastern
region) was about 2,06,000.

   From this brief description of the six churches which united, it
can be seen that at the time of the Union the total membership of the

Church of North India was approximately 6,50,000. This number has, over the past years, considerably increased not only by the addition of certain local congregations which joined the Church of North India after the 1970 union, but also an account of increased evangelistic ministry.

(d) The Basis of the Union

The basis on which the six churches united may be summed up as follows:

(i)   The recognition by the uniting churches that "the restoration of the visible unity of the Church on earth is the will of God" and that "the Holy Spirit is leading us to resolve the differences which at present separate us" (*Plan*, p. ix). Any move towards unity of churches is towards a fulfilment of Christ's prayer that they all may be one (Jn. 17:21).

The uniting churches also believed that the unity to which God was leading them would make the Church of North India a more effective instrument for His work, more eager and powerful to proclaim by word and deed the Gospel of Christ, filled with greater charity and peace, and enriched in worship and fellowship (*Plan*, p. ix).

(ii) Acceptance of the divinely inspired scriptures of the Old Testament and the New Testament as containing all things necessary for salvation and as the supreme and decisive standard of faith and conduct.

(iii) Acceptance of the creeds commonly known as the Apostles' Creed and the Nicene Creed as witnessing to and safeguarding the faith of the Church. These creeds are also recited in worship as acts of adoration and thanksgiving to God for his nature and for his redemptive acts, as well as in joyful affirmation of the faith which binds the worshippers together.

(iv) Acceptance of the two sacraments of Baptism and the Lord's Supper (or Holy Communion).

(v)   Mutual recognition and acceptance, by the uniting churches, of each other's Ministry.

(e) The Ordained Ministry

As has been mentioned above (in Section b) the inauguration of the Union included "The Representative Act of Unification of the Ministry". In this act, through prayer and a mutual laying-on-of-hands, the Church of North India received from God a unified ordained ministry acceptable to the whole church from the very beginning. It is the threefold ministry of bishops, presbyters and deacons within the broader framework of the "priesthood of all believers". The episcopate is both *historic* (i.e. in historic continuity with the early church) and *constitutional* (i.e. the bishops are appointed and they exercise their functions in accordance with the Consititution of the Church of North India). The Church of North India is not committed to any one particular theological interpretation of episcopacy, nor does it demand the acceptance of such an interpretation from its ministers or members.

In accepting this threefold ordained ministry it is the intention and determination of the Church of North India to maintain the unity of the ministry, but this does not involve any judgement upon the validity or regularity of any other form of the ministry.

The Fourth Synod of the Church of North India meeting on 4th October 1980, gave its approval to the ordination of women and resolved that, "The Church of North India admit women into the ordained ministry", and that "If in any diocese of the Church of North India the need arises for a woman to be ordained into the ministry of the Word and Sacraments the bishop concerned may do so with the approval of the Diocesan Council".

While valuing the threefold ordained ministry of bishops, presbyters and deacons, the Church of North India gives due place, within its life and work, to the ministry of the laity. Lay women and men have a place in the decision-making processes and administration of the Church at all levels.

(f) Baptism

As Baptist churches which practise only Believers' Baptism have united with other churches which also uphold the ancient practice of baptizing children, the Church of North India accepts both the Believers' Baptism and the Baptism of Children as two alternative practices. In the case of parents who desire that their children should be baptized only when they grow up and consciously make their own profession of faith, there is a provision for the "Blessing of Children" in their infancy. Admission to communicant membership of the baptized members is through "Confirmation or its equivalent rite."

(g) Organisation and Administration

Within India the Church of North India is organised on a territorial basis. It spreads over nearly two-thirds of the country north of Andhra Pradesh, and has a membership of over 7,00,000. It has a three-tier organisational and administrative structure–the Pastorate, the Diocese and the Synod.

The *Pastorate* is the basic organised unit of the Church, and this is where the real life of the Church is to be found in the unity and fellowship of believers, in the celebration of the sacraments and worship of God, in proclamation of the Gospel of Christ and participation in his mission, in bearing witness to God's justice, truth and love, and in numerous other forms and activities.

A pastorate may be a local congregation under the pastoral care of a presbyter, or it may be a cluster of two or more local congregations under the care of a presbyter-in-charge as its chairperson.

A *Diocese* is composed of several pastorates spread over a large area and it is placed under the pastoral care of a bishop. A diocese is administered by a diocesan council which is composed of all presbyters in the diocese who have not reached the age of retirement, and of elected representatives of the pastorates as well as some nominated and *ex-officio* members, presided over by the Bishop of the diocese. It meets at least once in two years.

At present there are 23 dioceses in the Church of North India, namely:

1.	Agra	13.	Eastern
2.	Amritsar		Himalayas(Darjeeling)
3.	Andaman and	14.	Gujarat
	Nicobar Islands	15.	Jabalpur
4.	Barrackpore	16.	Kolhapur
5.	Bhopal	17.	Lucknow
6.	Bombay	18.	Nagpur
7.	Calcutta	19.	Nasik
8.	Chandigarh	20.	North East
9.	Chotanagpur		India(Assam)
10.	Cuttack & Phulbani	21.	Patna
11.	Delhi	22.	Rajasthan
12.	Durgapur	23.	Sambalpur

The Diocesan Council plans and carries out its work through its executive committee and several other standing committees, such as the Stewardship Committee, Finance Committee, Property Committee, Liturgical Committee, Ministerial and Personnel Committee, Christian Life and Mission and Evangelism Committee, etc.

There are also Youth Fellowships and units of Women's Fellowship for Christian Service (WFCS) in the pastorates for youth and women's programmes with their respective committees at the level of the pastorate, the diocese and the synod.

The *Synod* is "The supreme, supervisory, legislative and executive body of the Church". It is "the organ of the whole Church, comprising all the dioceses" and is the "final authority in all matters pertaining to the Church" under the lordship of Christ. It is composed of all diocesan bishops, lay and ordained representatives of dioceses, and some nominated and *ex-officio* members. It meets once in three years and is presided over by the Moderator of the Church of North India who is elected by the synod from among the diocesan bishops for a term of three years. The synod's secretariat and other related offices are located at the headquarters of the Church of North India at "The CNI Bhavan", 16 Pandit Pant Marg, New Delhi 110001 (India).

The synod carries out its planning and work through its executive committee, its *Commissions* (on Theology, on Liturgy, on Religion and Life and the CNI Commission on Mission), its six *Boards* which control and guide the medical, educational and other institutions of the Church of North India (i.e. the Board of Social Services, Board of Agriculture, Board of Technical Education, Board of Higher Education, Board of Secondary Education, and the Board of Health Services), and nine *Standing Committees* (on Finance, Stewardship, Christian Life and Lay Activities, Literature and Mass Communication, Episcopal and Missionary Personnel, Law Procedures and Marriage, Committee of Reference, and the Judicial Committee). There are also the synodical committees of the Youth Fellowship and the Women's Fellowship for Christian Service which are responsible for planning and co-ordinating youth and women's programmes at the level of the synod (or whole church).

(h) Unity in Diversity

The Union has not meant uniformity nor absorption of one church by another. The united church cherishes and is enriched and strengthened by the diverse spiritual and liturgical heritage and experience of the former six churches which united. The unity in the Church of North India is a *unity in diversity*. Within the broader framework of the faith and order of the universal Church, the members of the Church of North India are assured of full freedom of conscience, belief and practice insofar as these do not conflict with the faith and order of the whole Church, and do not disrupt or endanger the fellowship of the Church. No form of worship or spirituality is imposed on any congregation. Over the past years new forms of worship and spirituality, a new understanding of unity and mission, and a greater commitment to go forward into deeper and wider union have been developing in the process of growing together in the Church of North India.

(i) United and Uniting

This *united* church is also a *uniting* church. In the words of the *Plan of Church Union in North India,* the former six uniting churches were "seeking the unity of the Spirit in the bond of peace, and earnestly desiring the coming of the day when, throughout the world, there shall be one flock and one shepherd" (p. viii). The inauguration of the Union on November 29, 1970, was not the end but a commitment to unity and uniting of churches in obedience to Christ's prayer and will. The Church of North India is in full inter-communion relationship with all churches with which the former six uniting churches were in communion at the time of the Union. Soon after the Union it was in full inter-communion relationship with the Church of South India and the Malankara Mar Thoma Syrian Church. At its first Synod which met at Jalandhar 20th-24th April, 1971, it adopted a general "Message to other Churches inviting them to wider union". Through this a clear overture was made to the Methodist Church in Southern Asia to resume union negotiations with them.

(j) The Motto

The motto of the Church of North India is *Unity, Witness, Service.* With this in focus the Church of North India continues to grow in unity, witness and service. The Union has brought to the united church not only the strength of numbers but also a new sense of mission, particularly in relation to the socio-economic, political, cultural and multi-religious context of contemporary India. Over the past years through the intermingling of traditions of the former churches a new 'CNI ethos' is developing. The Liturgical Commission has been hard at work and already the new CNI forms of worship and services for various occasions (e.g. Morning and Evening Worship, the Ordinal, the Lord's Supper, Believers' Baptism, Baptism of Children, Burial Service, Marriage Service and several other orders of services) have been produced in attractive booklet-forms. These have been widely used and are now also available in one 'Book of Worship' in English. The numerous medical, agricultural, educational, technical and social-service institutions of the CNI are the established channels of its service to the millions in the country, and these not only cater to the physical needs of the people but also work towards development of the marginalised, and the transformation of society. The Synodical Board of Social Services is involved in numerous development programmes, combating poverty, illiteracy, social injustice and exploitation, as well as in training leaders for the future.

(k) The CNI Badge and its meaning

A great deal of time, skill and devotion has gone into the design of the badge of the Church of North India.

The design is by Frank Wesley, the well known artist.

The circle in which the whole badge is enclosed is a symbol of eternity, for it is without beginning and without end. Christians are always to line against the background of eternity. They are among those who believe and remember that "behind the ebb and flow of things temporal, there stand the eternal verities."

Dominating the whole design is the Cross, the universally accepted badge of the Christian, reminding us of our Saviour, from whom we take our name. It stands for self giving and self-sacrifice, for patient endurance of suffering accepted for the sake of others; and because it was the Son of God who thus suffered and died for us, it is a golden cross, gold being the colour for godhead. Gold also suggests victory, reminding us that the Cross of Christ is the symbol of truimph, not of defeat.

The cross is set against a background of red, the colour of blood; and this again is a symbol of sacrifice and self-giving in the service of others. Red is also in liturgical usage the colour which stands for the Holy Spirit. It is the Holy Spirit who had led us into unity, and it is the Holy Spirit to whom we must still look for guidance. It is in the strength of the Holy Spirit, and only in his strength, that the Church and the individual Christian can hope to obey and serve God.

Behind the cross there is a lotus, dear to the heart of every Indian, the symbol of the spiritual quest of India, which we believe finds its final satisfaction only in the cross, and in Him who died on it.

The lotus is also the symbol of purity rising in all its own pure beauty out of mud beneath the water. This challenge of Purity is reinforced by the use of white for the flower and for the circle imposed upon it, "Blessed are the pure in heart, for they shall see God."

Within this inner circle of white there is set a chalice, as used in the Lord's Supper. Therein we receive sacramentally the atoning and redeeming blood of Christ, and so it is appropriately set against a background of red. But the chalice itself is gold, for the sacrament is God's gift of his own life.

The chalice is set at the very centre of the whole badge, to teach us that worship and sacrament are at the centre of Christian living. God must be the centre of our lives. The first and great commandment is to love God; and that love, coming from a creature to his Creator, must find expression in worship.

But there is a second commandment: "Thou shalt love thy neighbour as thyself." Therefore, lest our very worship should become selfish and self-centred, we are continually to go out from the worship at the heart of our lives into the world, and use the grace we have received in the service of our fellowmen.

Last, but not least, as we move out from the centre, we come back to the outer circle, and there we are given the three key words Unity, Witness, Service. The Church of North India is to seek and work and pray for the unity of all who bear the name of Christ. At the same time she has to use the unity which God has given her in order that she may more faithfully and more effectively bear witness to her faith, and may give herself to the service of all without distinction, after the example of her Servant Lord.

We must be extremely grateful to Frank Wesley who gave us this splendid badge. What a wealth of meaning and teaching it has for us!

(I) Priorities Towards 2000 A.D.

Spiritual Renewal.

Unity within the Church of North India and with other Churches.

Mission and Evangelism.

Development of Christian leadership.

Socio-economic and political concerns, particularly the struggles of the oppressed and marginalised sections of society such as women, dalits, indigenous communities (tribals), etc., for their self development, dignity and wholesome life.

Dialogue with people of other faiths.

Structural changes leading to decentralisation, democratisation, and devolution of power.

Indigenisation and contextualisation of life, work and worship of the Church.

Self-reliance in personnel and financial resources.

CHAPTER 1

"I believe ...."

Being a Christian is exciting. There's lots to do and we sense that we are going places with God. As most of us, when we are going on a·tour or changing residence, try to find out some details of the journey and plan accordingly, so those who seek to follow Christ, will want to be sure that they are 'going places' in the right direction and in the right attitude of mind.

Many of us repeat one or other of the Creeds quite regularly. (Of course, we never, never say the words thoughtlessly! –or do we?). There is no denying the worth of these Creeds because they give the bare bones of our faith. Put together and condensed by early Christians, these short statements of faith can be easily memorised. Many of the earliest Christians could not read or write, and many had no copy of the New Testament books or the Old Testament Jewish scriptures available, but they could retain the Creed in their minds and could find in it a check list of what they believed.

Ideas about God and practical details of daily human living should hold together, but the ideas have to come first. Look at any decent building and you will find that before the building started there were plans drawn up. The architect first had ideas about the building, then sketched these out and modified them, then drew up plans. Only then did the building commence. Something of the architect is seen in the finished structure. In the same way the Creeds condense the ideas underlying God's plan of salvation for mankind. The life we live is the building taking shape. The Creeds help to describe what God was, and is doing through Jesus Christ.

Shall we be wasting time, if we look at one of the creeds, e.g. the Apostles' Creed? You may have studied this already, but it is worth looking at this again to remind ourselves of the truth behind the Creed.

The Creeds, like the Bible, are aids to faith and for life. They are never substitutes for personal faith. It is possible to know the theories about God without abiding in a living truthful relationship with God. So, as we study the teaching of the Apostles' Creed, let us realise we are looking at the condensed truth, the skeleton of Christian ideas about God. All the aspects of the Creed need to be fleshed out.

We say we believe in God the Father? What do we understand by the word 'Father'? God is Spirit, whereas all the other 'fathers' we know have had bodies. We talk about God the Father because Jesus referred to God as Father. As a youngster of twelve he asked, "Did you not understand I must be in my Father's house?" Before the cross he said, "I am going to my Father and your Father", and on the cross he pleaded, "Father, forgive them..." and "Father, into your hands I commit my spirit." Here is Jesus relating to God the Father and allowing us to also call God 'Father'. Not forgetting the role of the mother also, let us remember that a father creates his family and gives them his name. He plans for them and should care for them. It may well be that you could quote a hundred examples of human fathers who fall short of the mark of responsible fatherhood, but that does not affect the truth that parent/child relationship is the nearest human relationship that we find on earth. It determines who is 'next of kin' to us and what genes we have. So Jesus, needing to speak of the astounding relationship between himself and the God who sent him, used the best term he could find in the Jewish language, and the term was 'Abba', 'Father' or 'Papa'. The word had already been used to express the divine/human relationship between Israel and the God who had been and continued to be active for their salvation, e.g. Moses in Deuteronomy 32:6 asks, "Is He not your father, who created you, who made you and established you?" and the prophet Jeremiah speaks for God, in 31:9 saying "for I am a father to Israel."

It may be a puzzle to some to talk of God our Creator in terms of a Person rather than an impersonal Force. We admit the puzzle, but have to state that just as an animal is of greater wonder than a rock, so a human being is more than just an animal—even though some human beings may seem more like animals in their habits and activities. Personality is a concept that represents the 'higher' side of a human being's make up. She or he is a thinking, planning, scheming, volitional unit who can use the personal pronoun 'I' from earliest days; "I want...", "I like...", "I shall...". If we try to think in terms of a purely spiritual force, shall we invent a term such as 'Divine Electricity'? Such a force may have an effect on me, but there is no Person to Person relationship in it. It is an impersonal force, whereas the God we find written of in the Bible and spoken of by Jesus and encountered by ourselves is a Person. God is Spirit but also a Person. Each one of us as we come on the stage of life relates to Him as a Person and He to us. To know that the divine 'bodiless' Being is also a Person who desires to help me relate personally to Him—with an eternal relevance—is mind boggling! We accept that I am bewildered by it; I am dazzled by its prospect; but I am also profoundly joyful at the possibility and find that in order to accomplish this development in the purpose of the Creator, "the Word became flesh and dwelt among us". When I consider Jesus of Nazareth, I see God at work as in no other instance, creating a bridge and removing barriers so that you and I can each call ourself 'a child of God'.

Moving on in the Creed to the words 'His Son', we note that Jesus repeatedly referred to himself as 'Son', most often as 'Son of man', but did not deny the popular title of Messiah 'Son of David' or even the acclamation 'Son of God' (see Matthew 21:15 where children in the temple praised Him; and John 1:49 where Nathanael makes his discovery). This term 'Son' was the best He could choose to describe himself. If He had called himself 'Cousin-brother to God' or 'Handiwork of God' it would not have conveyed the truth adequately. Jesus must have felt the Father/Son relationship was the most appropriate term available, and one which was universally understood so He used it. Because He used it, we use it!

This does not mean that there are no questions for us to ask, no problems to tackle. There may be many. Our Muslim friends question, "How is it possible for a divine Being to have a human son?" Co-habitation between a Creator Spirit and a young woman must seem nonsense! We can appreciate such a question and honestly respond, "We cannot explain the mechanics!" But there are lots of things we cannot explain though we know they happen. Ordinary human reproduction can be described, examined by an electron microscope, pictured and detailed, –this happens, then that happens, then the body develops, then the brain is there, then the eyes, etc., etc. –but it still does not explain how the gift of life is passed on. The joining of two cells happens before our eyes, but the fact that it happens does not explain it. How a new creation with a physical and mental content, and a spiritual aspect also, can come about from two separate beings is a mystery, even though it happens a thousand times a day. We ultimately have to say, 'This is a biological fact of life, and because we know it happens we accept it.' A human birth is a picture of a spiritual fact. Somehow the God who is Spirit and the Source of all life communicated to Mary of Nazareth that which made her supernaturally pregnant. Using her body, God 'the Father' brought 'the Son' into the form of a human being. In this act He, the divine Creator, bridged the gap between Himself and Creation in a new and startling revelation. Look at a child and you will see something of the parents. Consider Jesus and you will find yourself considering God Himself.

In this step into faith the work of the Holy Spirit is known by each one of us. Somehow the Person that is God comes near me to create a hunger for life and for the truth. He introduces me to experiences of God, often with the help of other human persons, and I latch on to new discoveries and find out more of God. "This is a delusion and a mystery!" some may say. Mystery, yes; for who can fathom all the ways of God? –but delusion, never! even though it is in ourselves only that we know such a transaction is taking place. The work of the Holy Spirit can be known in other ways also; –as we learn of the saving experience in the lives of our fellows, or in His influence on humankind through great and small events on the canvas of world history.

It is because of a Christian's personal experience of God the Father and readiness to accept the revelation of God in His Son, Jesus, and to proceed on that basis lifelong with the help of the Holy Spirit, that he or she can say, "I believe in....." This act of submission in faith to God is a basis for living in co-operation with the God who is and who always will be. The Christian life is an adventure. Not everything is known. Not every Christian has the same joys or sorrows, but this relationship with God in Christ is a continuing experience and is meant to continue beyond the experience of human death.

Before we turn to consideration of the resurrection we need to think about the death of Christ. "He ... died and was buried," says the Creed, and that sounds fairly final! It is indeed meant to convey that very fact. The one who came into this life by the process of being born as we are born, went out of it by dying as we die. All of us, as and when we have to face death, can do so knowing that Jesus went that way. When we pray through Him to the Father for those facing death, we know that He understands because He has also faced death.

There are some who say "Jesus went to Kashmir (or elsewhere) and died there," or "The man on the cross was not Jesus! Jesus slipped away and someone else was crucified." Such notions may spring from a basic feeling that a divine person cannot die. In the early centuries there were philosophers who preached that Jesus was only a ghostly figure. It was said that the ghostly being, Jesus, only gave the appearance of dying. But you cannot drive nails into the hands and feet of a ghost! The earliest Gospel writers underline the real facts and are quite clear, as also are the Creeds, that Jesus Christ really died and that He died one of the cruelest and most painful deaths it is possible to experience.

Much has been written about the meaning of the cross and the sacrificial death of Jesus Christ, and this book does not give scope for an in-depth study. The subject is too vast. We will simply point to the fact that the Jews had been given a sacrificial system in which desire for atonement for sins was expressed from the human side by sacrifice. In the crucifixion of Christ we have not only an example of the lengths to which sinful human beings are prepared to go in getting rid of one who confronted their sinful nature, but we have the supreme example of the sacrifice of life, the innocent for the guilty, the perfect man being sacrificed on behalf of all mankind.

Let us also be aware that Christ's suffering is a great comfort to those who suffer. The Saviour of the world has experienced the bitterest pain. The pain that we can know is known to Him also. However terrible may be our suffering, we can know that He has shared such agony.

Sometimes people may ask us, "What happened to those who died before Jesus came?" We need to answer with care, because none of us can pronounce on what we do not know. But we can point to such a statement in the Creed as "He descended to the dead," and to verses of scripture such as 1 Peter 3:19. God in His mercy has ensured that the gospel is made available to those who had died before Jesus' coming.

This leads us to the topic of Resurrection, which is a continuing of personal life beyond the grave. What little we know about it derives from the resurrection of Jesus. It is one of the 'New' things that come into actuality because of Jesus. We accept the resurrection because Jesus rose from the dead. This resurrection is not a 'return to life' like a recovery from a coma. It is a personal life on the other side of the grave. The Resurrection Body of Jesus was somehow the same as before, because his hands and feet were still marked by the nails and spear wounds; but also somehow different because (a) He was not always recognised when He appeared, and (b) his body was not restricted to time/space as it had been before. Because of these differences, after the resurrection his body is sometimes called his 'glorified' body. The Resurrection is also a proof that what happens 'this' side of the grave somehow affects that which continues on the 'other' side. It has a logical 'cause and effect' sort of link; i.e. What I do 'here' I carry with me. I am a moral being and my contribution to life, be it for good or for evil, does not become automatically wiped out by my death. Jesus taught certain things about the resurrection—see Matthew 22:30 and John 5: 28-29—and because He taught it and showed it, we can believe in it. This does not mean we know all the answers about it.

'He ascended into heaven' is a simple statement that Christ returned to where He had previously been with the Father. There is a certain difficulty for us these days about the word 'ascended' in the sense of 'going up', though this truly represents the thought in scripture such as John 6:62; John 20:17; and Acts 1:2. Astronauts circle the earth and astronomers study the galaxies. People gazing up in Central America are gazing in approximately the opposite direction to those 'gazing up' in India! So no longer can we be content with the idea of a flat earth like a *thali* and a heaven like a basin placed upside down to cover it. Even so, we who are human beings with a limited life span still retain the word 'infinity'. There is still an eternal dimension to which we relate while we are in time and space. There is a state of being which is beyond our present earthly state. That realm, where God is, where He who is Spirit exists outside of time and beyond human manipulation, but not beyond communication, is heaven.

It may be helpful in this matter to refer to a theatrical stage. Sometimes a stage is divided into two by a gauze curtain. By cleverly lighting the front of the stage only, the actors in the front area are the only ones seen. When the back portion is lit, then the back half of the stage and the people on it are also seen. This may seem a totally inadequate illustration of 'heaven', but it may help us to sense that heaven is not necessarily a matter of distance in metres and miles, but of a state of being which we do not see at the moment. In whatever way we may think of heaven, that is where Christ is, and His activity is consistent with the life He led on earth.

The apostle Paul wrote of the risen Christ interceding for us (Romans 8:34) and the writer to the Hebrews (7:25) remembering the priestly role of Christ says He always lives to make intercession for those who draw near to God through him. So we are reminded of Jesus Christ's sacrificial death being for our salvation. John in the book of Revelation (5:6) also has the vision of the Lamb of God in heaven, Jesus, still having the marks of crucifixion on him. His sacrificial atonement for mankind is still effective!

In His parables in Matthew 25 and His teaching in Mark 13 for example, Jesus speaks of His second coming. Scripture points to a 'second coming' of Christ, and nothing in modern cosmology alters this truth. If He came the first time, He can come a second time. The second coming seems to be an important step towards completion of God's purpose in man's redemption. It involves the accountability of all mankind before God. Here the final audit takes place and judgement is involved for each one of us. This is a daunting prospect for us all, but, thank God, we who trust in Christ now can trust him at that time also.

The 'How' or 'When' of this Second Coming we do not know. Indeed, we are not meant to know, see verses such as Mark 13:32; Matthew 24:36; and Acts 1:7; so this need not unduly worry us. But we have to be watchful, prepared for Christ's coming at any time.

One of the 'New' things which the first coming of Christ initiated was the Church, i.e those 'called out' of mankind in general to be a task force, ready to relate to their Commanding Officer day by day and willing to carry out his orders. The Jewish nation had been a chosen people, selected from many nations to be particularly aware of God's grace, to know God's power, trust His promises and respect His truth. The writings of lawgivers, psalmists and prophets which we find in the Old Testament indicate the success which God achieved with the Children of Israel. These writings also indicate clearly how often that success was marred by repeated acts of defiance in the face of God and by disobedience to his principles. The failures of Israel are not facts to be crowed about' by Christians or by others, but rather should cause us to ask honestly, "Would we have done any better?" or, more appropriately, "Have we done any better?" One big succcess with Israel was that out of this nation God selected a small number of people to prepare a cradle for the Messiah. One big failure was Israel's ignoring of her ministry to all nations. When God called Abram (see Genesis 12:1-3) part of the announcement was "and by you all the families of the earth shall be blessed." This purpose is re-stated more than once (see Genesis 18:18; 22:18; 26:4; 28:14). The idea of being a 'chosen people' led to the wrong assumption that they were chosen for their own worthiness (though see Deuteronomy 9:6 etc) and the aspect of world-wide service became warped. By the time that Messiah came the Jews were so far off-centre that they did not recognise him but rather resisted and refused him. It became clear that a New Israel would have to be established because in God's design seen in the ministry and gospel of Jesus, his death and mediation was clearly for ALL mankind. So the Church began. The original band of apostles and disciples formed a nucleus which showed signs of expanding even before the crufixion of our Lord. After his resurrection and the out-pouring of the Holy Spirit there was a positive explosion that showed the Rule of God extended far beyond national boundaries. The Church spread rapidly, though at first it did not call itself 'The Church'. 'Followers of the Way' seems to have been one of the names given to Christians (Christ-ones). Luke in the Acts of the Apostles uses the term 'Church' early on, the basic meaning of which is 'Those who are called out'. We note that an ever increas-ing community of people was selected from all nations by God to know His truth in Christ, to be helped by the Holy Spirit to be His servants for the good of mankind. The words "all nations" indicate the church is a world-wide body, and another word for 'world-wide' is 'catholic'. We need to clearly understand that in the Creeds we are not saying that we believe in one world-wide Roman Catholic Church, but rather in The World-wide Christian Church composed of all Christians.

That the Church has been a success in this God-given purpose of serving others is open to argument. There have been all too many occasions where the Church is purely self-interested, unresponsive, keen to codify its own rules and regulations but careless about lov-ing obedience. Even so, it does seem that God had persevered with the Church as He has also persevered with the people of Israel; and you voluntarily joined the great community of those who trust Christ for redemption and seek to serve Him. So God is still active. May He use you to correct some of the errors other people have made.

The remainder of the Apostles' Creed points to other important items of faith. They are:

The Communion of Saints, i.e., there is a bond in the 'new' community of the Church which is not only world-wide but which endures. We are at one with all who follow Christ. One of the as-pects of the Lord's Table or Holy Communion is that this table extends through the centuries. It also extends into the future and points to the final honouring of God and His Christ at which the

Church will also be present. No wonder this is pictured as a tremendous occasion, a sort of heavenly Wedding Feast.

The Forgiveness of Sins–which gives a new hope for sinners. We are all sinners. Not one of us is perfect, but 'in Christ' we can trust God to forgive us. We do not have to go through life wondering whether we can be forgiven. Through Jesus God provides a way of forgiveness for us. This can easily lead to a careless attitude to sin, i.e., "If God is going to forgive my sin anyway, then let me sin and enjoy all the unrestrained delights of this life and then ask for forgiveness. If God loves me so much, He will love me 'at the end' whatever I do." That is human sinful nature looking for selfish advantage. Go that way and before long sin has lost any meaning! It fails to take into account the serious nature of sin–which is "being cut off from God". If we want to be cut off from God 'now', we are preparing ourselves to be cut off for ever, and that is a description of Hell!

The Life Everlasting results from a bonding through grace and faith between God and the believer. We do not know all about it, which is not surprising because we are 'here' and not yet 'there', but it is reflected throughout the scripture and helps make moral sense of the apparent injustices of this life we live on earth.

So much for the 'theory' of life as a Christian sees it. What about the practical nitty-gritty? Supposing the Creed is right and OK, what effect does this have on daily life? What do we have to DO? This we shall tackle in the following chapters. The aspects of the Christian life which will be covered cannot be exhaustive, but hopefully these will be enough to both challenge and encourage you as you progress along the path of discipleship.

Questions

1. Why is it good to repeat the Creeds regularly?
2. What difficulties, if any, do you have in saying the Creeds?
3. Is there any aspect of our Christian faith that does not feature in the creeds that you feel should be included?

4. A Roman Catholic, a member of the Church of North India, a member of a Pentecostal church will all accept the Creed as a statement of their faith. How can we be so different and yet claim to share the same beliefs?

5. The Creeds say nothing about the Ten Commandments. Do these have any relevance to the Christian Faith?

CHAPTER 2

Keeping Fit

God is coaching us like athletes in training. Daily exercise helps us to realise our potential, as each athlete has to engage in the training programme. It cannot all be left to the coach. So what directions and help does God give us?

One is the Bible, a written record of progressive revelation. Most of it we can easily understand, and we need not despair if there are parts that are difficult. Of course it is quite possible for an illiterate person to be a Christian, but to be able to personally read about things that God has worked out in the world and the processes He uses is a distinct advantage. Let us take a look at what kind of book the Bible is.

The Bible is not simply one book. It is more like two shelves of books made into one volume. The first shelf contains the books of the Old Testament, from Genesis to Malachi. These were originally written in Hebrew and specially concern God's dealing with the Jewish nation. The second shelf, with the books from Matthew to Revelation, is the New Testament. It was originally written mostly in Greek by those who knew Jesus during His earthly life and after His resurrection. Because Jesus was a Jew and knew the Old Testament which contains details of God's preparation for Christ's coming for all people including the Jewish nation, we find it helpful to study the Old Testament as well as the New.

You and I can find a Bible and read it quite easily in our own language, but it was not always so. For example, English translations were made only about 400 years ago, and that after quite a struggle against priestly authorities in the Church. Even today some people have no translation in their own mother tongue.

It is helpful to know the over-all pattern of the books of the Bible. There are 39 in the Old Testament which are placed in four sections: (1) The five books of Moses, Genesis to Deuteronomy, tell the Jewish account of creation and of our universal ancestors. Then comes the early history and laws of the Jewish people from the time of Abraham to the death of Moses. It is a fascinating story of a great family which grew into a nation. The story is told from the point of view of the people's relationship with God and the way He dealt with them in times of war, famine, disobedience and success. (2) The next section deals with more history of the Jews, giving an account of what happened in the reign of each leader or king, good or bad. (3) Contains a number of books of prose and poetry which have a religious theme; Job, Psalms, Proverbs, Ecclesiastes and Song of Songs. (4) Finally there are books of the major and the minor prophets who spoke up for God in times of difficulty in national life, always calling the people to be faithful to God and show justice to their fellow human beings.

The books on the second shelf, the 27 that make up the New Testament, start with the four Gospels. These are four accounts of Jesus' earthly life, death and resurrection, written by different people. These are followed by the Acts of the Apostles, which continues Luke's account of what happened after the resurrection and tells of Jesus' return to heaven, the coming of the Holy Spirit and the work of the apostles establishing early groups of believers. After Acts comes a large number of letters of advice to the churches by Paul and others. Finally, the Book of Revelation contains messages for a group of churches and a vision of the future.

When people become Christians, they usually make it a habit to read a few verses from the Bible every day. Sometimes they attempt to read through a book, bit by bit, and sometimes just dip into the Bible wherever it happens to open. While this may be better than nothing, it certainly is not using the Bible in the best way. It is a great help to use some form of Bible Reading Notes where each day there is a portion of scripture for reading and then comments about it. Such comments made by other Christian people are usually a help because we can benefit from their experience and wisdom. However, we have to let the Bible speak for itself. We have to let God lead our individual thoughts as we read the scriptures. We believe God led people to write down certain truths and facts which had come to their notice through their own experiences. Often our experiences resemble theirs and God has something to say to us. Even if we disagree with the comment, at least we have had the benefit of thinking about it, and that counts for a lot.

What if the Bible seems to have a standard of perfection that asks too much of us! Sometimes it may seem that way, for the Bible is full of examples of what is right compared to what is wrong, and it all seems to be a matter of black and white. But isn't it to be expected that, if our God is holy and perfect, His standards are like that too? Yet the experience of the people God used to write the scriptures is, that God uses them despite their defects, He is active for mankind's salvation. He seeks to include us as active participants in His plan, even though we have our shortcomings. He is a *saving* God and He is 'in charge'. So the thing to do is face up to what He tells us. We may honour Him, or argue with Him; reject His advice, or attempt to ignore Him, but that does not stop Him endeavouring to change us as we need to be changed. We all need to learn not to be careless about life, be it our own life or that of other people. We have to take care how we affect others and how we relate to others or legislate for them. But thank God we have not to be obsessed with 'legal' niceties, but with a living relationship with Him. We walk through life in the power of God and ask Him daily to help us on our way.

It is possible to read right through the Bible a book at a time, but sometimes the going gets tough and, anyway, the order of books in the Bible is not arranged like chapters in a novel. This is where Bible Reading Notes are a help. They usually follow a theme or a book of the Bible and make comments on the background of the passage as well as on its meaning. The reader is left to apply the lesson to personal situations. In this way we can share the writer's insights and learn from another's mistakes and opportunities. This means we have to pay out something every quarter or every year, for such Notes have to be produced and paid for. However such a payment is surely not asking too much of any us. Most of us spend much more on snacks or postage than we do on Bible Studies!

What is the best time to read the Bible? This depends on our life style. If our job means we leave home very early, it may be difficult to do anything more than read a verse or two and have a brief prayer. If, however, it is mid-morning before we leave our home, then a time before or after breakfast is possible. Sometimes it seems that the only time is 'last thing at night', but the trouble is that at the end of the day tiredness makes us slack about our devotions. It is so easy for such an inclination to become a habit. For those whose routine is a very busy one, it is necessary to block off time for God. It is better to have ten minutes regularly each day than keep waiting for something better to turn up. It probably won't! Of course, it's almost certain that something will then happen to distract us from 'that ten minutes'. Do not let that fact put you off. It's a good sign! The powers of evil always try to distract us. If your devotional time is interrupted, do not let that put you off. Get back to routine as soon as possible, –and note what interrupts you. God may use the interruption to give you some hint of what needs to be done!

Aim to start each day with a portion of scripture and prayer. 'Bible before breakfast' is a good rule. It enables God to direct our endeavours. If God uses the scriptures to point out to us some error which needs putting right, let's not feel disappointed that God has caught us out! After all, that is what we would surely expect if the Word of God (as we sometimes call the Bible) is truly one way in which God gets through to us. The Bible is full of situations that compare with those we are going through. These were written for our guidance, because what happened to others may happen to us, so it's up to us to let the Spirit of God inform our minds through the words we read, and so let God shape us and our future.

Is ten minutes long enough for devotions? The answer is 'Yes' and 'No'! Nothing is laid down as to how long prayers should be. A sincere ten minutes with God is more satisfying that twenty minutes of rambling thoughts. But as there is reason to communicate with God about many things, then ten minutes will soon run out.

Is there a correct posture for prayer? It is quite possible for God to communicate with us while we are sitting on a bus or walking in the street. A hospital patient may have no choice except to pray to God whilst stretched out in bed. So, in one way, as long as we realise God is present, prayer can be anywhere. Even so, most find it better to kneel or sit in a quiet place, and we often close our eyes–though, if you find yourself going to sleep, pray with your eyes open!

What is the best 'order' for prayer? A good guide is 'God first, others next, self last.' Putting God first is quite a challenge because words of praise do not come easily. But there is no reason why we should not use words from the Bible such as the beginning of Psalms 8 or 9. Other Psalms like No. 100, 103, 104, 105, all provide useful prayers—as does the heavenly praise in Revelation 4: 8-11 or 15: 3-4. It is also possible to use prayers that others have composed. They seem to say things better than we càn. Thanks to God follows quickly on 'Praise' and there are lots and lots of things we can include on our list—intelligence, skills, loving relations, gifts such as sight, hearing, ability to learn, design, communicate, and ABOVE ALL of course, thanks for the salvation revealed in Jesus.

It is not surprising if, having become aware of the presence of God through Praise, the next feeling we get is of unworthiness. So prayers of confession and repentance may well follow or mingle with Praise and Thanks. John 21: 15-19 can help us, or maybe Psalms 32 and 51. Repent and confess your sins to God and ask Him to forgive you.

Prayers for 'others' are never-ending. There are so many 'other' concerns, and all of them deserving a place in our prayers. Probably it is best to select a few each day for special mention, e.g. family and close relatives, people who have special needs, people who are specially our responsibility, etc. A good idea is to have a written list of such friends and needs, and to keep this list in our Bible. To mention a few each day is easy. Others can be added from time to time and, when necessary, items can be crossed off the list.

Prayers for self come naturally, but we have to remember that God is quite aware of each situation we face. What we need is not so much an in-depth description of the situation to present to God, but the ability to discern what is needed, what our attitude should be, and to persevere in the right way.

Let us remember also that sometimes God's answer is 'No'. This can give us acute disappointment, especially when the things we have been asking for seem to us so clearly right, but we have to let God know best. Probably Joseph in the Old Testament could have rightly asked God to get him out of the pit into which his jealous brothers had placed him, or later in Egypt, he could have rightly requested release from prison because the charges fabricated against him were unjust and malicious. But God let him be taken into slavery and suffer horribly so that, in the end, he could personally learn the leasson 'You meant it for evil, but God meant it for good!' and could become the means of saving his entire family–and of setting the scene for the next step in God's plan of mankind's salvation. It is a process in discipleship to accept His 'No' and to trust Him all the same.

So many of our concerns are selfish, –what we want in the way of money, friendship, provision, wisdom, etc., –and there is nothing wrong in that. God has made us with the instinct of self-preservation. If we didn't have that, we'd soon be dead while crossing the road! But we do need to remind ourselves again and again that God does not run this world for our 'selfish' benefit. His purposes do include us, yes! –but His purposes are multiple and vast. We should not expect Him to fit His designs around our self-centredness, but we have to have His purposes at the centre of our endeavour. We shall get far more satisfaction that way!

Most people have difficulty in concentrating during personal prayer time. It is so easy if we are 'thinking' a prayer, for our thoughts to get side-tracked. We find to our horror that one moment we are praising our Creator and the next we are wondering what sort of vegetables we want for our next meal. It does help to 'speak' our prayers. It can also be helpful to read our prayers from a book (and mean them) or to memorise some prayers and pray these (and mean them). In any case, if and when we find ourselves wandering we have to get back on course. When we are speaking to our boss or to a friend, we concentrate on what we are saying, so when we realise that in prayer we are speaking to One who is both our boss and our friend–and very much more!, it is right that we should sincerely pay attention. After all, if we are asking God for 'action', let us at least pay Him the respect of waiting upon Him for his answer.

Prayer partners can help our concentration. Two or three good friends can be prayer partners together. A husband and wife can be prayer partners. The need is to decide together on time, place and day. Then take it in turns to lead in prayer. Sharing in this way helps us to pray meaningfully. We help each other. Such prayer partnerships can be part of a local church's expression of fellowship. However, two words of caution need to be said. One is that prayer partners need to preserve absolute confidentiality regarding what is said in such a group. We cannot share our inner thoughts freely, if our partners are going to broadcast them. Second, we need to avoid using the sort of words or phrases which we think others want to hear. We tend to slip into a habit of using favourite words and phrases or sighing and halleluyahing repeatedly. That we should say 'Halleluyah' ("God be praised") and mean it, is fine, but to say 'Halleluyah' out of habit without meaning it is anything but fine. We need not worry about our grammar or correct pronunciation. God reads our minds and knows us! "Even before a word is on my tongue, you know it, Lord." So prayertime has plenty of scope.

We have been considering Bible reading and praying, but the other side of this is doing–which takes up the other 95% of our day! An athlete may benefit a lot by theory or studying a video of other sportspeople, but there is no substitute for action and practice. So we must practice what we preach, or rather we must practice what the Bible preaches. If and as we fail, we have to get up and make another attempt. An Olympic record may be established on a 'one-off' occasion in front of crowds of people, but before that the athlete had gone through the routine a thousand times. So keep practising, and if you slip and fall on your face (no doubt to the amusement of many of your friends) don't lie rolling in the dirt, get up, let God dust you down, and try again.

Questions

1. How can the Bible which was written 2,000 years ago, have any relevance for my life today?

2. I am one of a large family and I do not have a room of my own. How can I find a time and place for prayer and Bible reading?

3. List some of the things you have found helpful in your devotional time, e.g. Study notes, prayer lists; and also things that distract you. Share and discuss.

4. "I do not have a set time for prayer, but pray as I feel led at any time and wherever I am." Discuss.

CHAPTER 3

The Church : My Church

In the prologue to this book we looked briefly at the history of the Church of North India and noted something of the various denominations that came together to form the C.N.I. Now that you have become a member of this Church, for you the C.N.I. has become 'My' Church. However, you will meet other people and will probably have friends who are not members of C.N.I. who will speak of the church they attend as 'My' Church. They may tell you of the different ways in which they worship and the different emphases they put on particular doctrines. So then, is there more than one Church? Or, if there is only one Church, how is 'My Church' part of 'The Church'?

It is worthwhile remembering that the word 'church' in the New Testament has the basic idea of a group of people who are 'called out' of society in general in order to do a particular job. It was in such a way that a city would have a group of fighting men 'called out' to form its army. The word 'church' is found only in two verses in the Gospels. First, after Jesus had asked the disciples "Who do you say that I am?" and Peter had answered, "You are the Christ." Jesus said, "On this rock I will build my church." (Matt. 16:18). Through faith in Jesus as Saviour, God is able to build His Church, Jesus Himself being the foundation laid by God (1 Cor. 3:11). In Matt. 18:17 the word church is again used, obviously referring to a group of believing disciples. When Jesus said these words, there were no church buildings, and no formal church organisation. Jesus had indeed 'called out' of the people of Israel a small group of people who accepted Him as anointed by God for the purpose of being a Saviour, but organisation would develop as the number of believers grew and the Gospel spread out into many countries. However widely the Church spread, the foundation would remain the same, –the acknowledging of Jesus Christ as Lord.

Church History is a fascinating subject. As we study it we wonder at the way the Church has grown and spread, but at the same time we will feel ashamed at some of the things that have been done in the name of Christ and sadness at the divisions that have arisen within God's people. We can detect differences of opinion between apostles like Peter and Paul (see Galatians 2:11; and 2 Peter 3:16;) nevertheless, the promise that Jesus gave to the early disciples that "the gates of hell shall not prevail"against His Church have proved to be true and the Church has grown so that believers are to be found in almost every country of the world. If we visit another country and attend a service, we might find it very different from worship in our 'home' congregation. Different cultures have brought different customs into church worship. Different periods of history have introduced different emphases into doctrines, but where Christ is acknowledged as Lord, the Christian scriptures followed as God's Word, and His lordship demonstrated by obedience and service, there is His Church.

The Church is like a family and when we become part of the Church we become part of this family. We are brothers and sisters in Christ. We may differ in many ways. We may hold strong views about the rightness of our own doctrinal emphasis or style of worship, but we are still part of one family into which we have been adopted (see Galatians, 4: 5-7). The Church of which you have become a part is greater than C.N.I.

But how can we know that all who claim to be followers of Jesus Christ are really true believers? What about heresy? In its history the Church has had to face this problem again and again. It was in AD 451 that the leaders of the Church at a great Council in Nicea accepted what has become known as the Nicene Creed. This and other such Creeds have been used down the centuries to state in simple terms the basic beliefs that identify Christians. When we recite the creeds we are reminding ourselves of the faith which unites all true believers in the Lord Jesus Christ. It is by the truth contained in the Bible and the creeds that we can measure, as far as it is humanly possible, whether or not any particular group of people can claim to be Christians. We do well to keep in mind the words of

Jesus Himself, "By this all men will know that you are my disciples, if you have love for one another." Creeds without love to go with them do not represent a Christian way of life.

If then, the Church is made up of all who believe in the Lord Jesus Christ, where does 'My' church fit into this? Is it necessary to belong to a church? Is it necessary to attend church services regularly? There are a number of reasons why it is good and right to belong to a local church fellowship. Four are suggested below. You may be able to think of others.

(i)   It is through the local church that we experience the reality of being part of the whole universal Church. It would be a strange family in which each member lived an entirely separate life with no concern for the other family members. Throughout the Bible God shows His concern for His people and His desire that we should care for each other. It is by meeting together that we become aware of the needs of God's people locally as well as ways in which He is to be served throughout the world.

(ii)   When we become communicant members of the Church we are just beginning on the path of discipleship. We are like students who have just joined college. We are excited to have reached this stage; we are excited about the new vistas of knowledge that are opening up before us, excited at the thought of new friendships to be made, at the new experiences of self-discovery we can expect to have. Joining the local church is a bit like that. Any student will tell you that there is much more to be gained by attending a college to study than to staying at home and trying to learn the subjects from books. In the interchange of ideas, in the heat of debates, in the opportunities to question experienced lecturers, in all these ways a student's mind and understanding develops and grows. In our local churches we have opportunity to learn from experienced leaders. Through sermons, study groups, discussions that arise with fellow members, we grow in our understanding of the Christian way of life. We find out what is meant by fellowship as we worship together. We learn of needs and are challenged about what we can do to help meet those needs. Around us are people who can support and guide us when we face problems in our own discipleship. Perhaps most of all, as we share in the sacraments of the Church our spirits are nourished by God's Holy Spirit. The illustration of a bucket of glowing coals is a good one. While the lumps of coal are all together they burn brightly. Take out a lump and put it by itself and it will quickly cool off.

(iii) All of us have to fight the battle of gettting on in this world and this can become a very selfish operation. Our time, our energy, our thinking can all become geared to this matter of personal success in the very competitive society of today. We begin to see our needs, our ambitions as all that really matters. The local church offers a balance to this. The wording of the prayers that we say together week by week, as well as the special days that we observe, serve to keep us mindful of the needs of others. It may be that visitors from overseas or missionaries from our own country tell us of the work that they are doing and how they need our prayer and financial support. We need these challenges, if we are not to become totally self-centred individuals.

(iv) Another good reason for going to church is in order to make friends. Friendships are important. They can be lifelong and a great influence on us. We need to choose our best friends with care. As we move from school to college, from college into employment, or from one neighbourhood to another, we shall be part of a group of people thrown together by circumstances. Some friends will be very supportive of us and will help us maintain a Christian walk of life. Others will want us to do things that compromise our loyalty to Christ. Not everyone we meet in a church fellowship will necessarily be a wholesome friend, so we make our choices with care, but it can be reasonably expected that within our church fellowship we shall develop friendships that will be loyal and lifelong. Good and lasting friendships which begin in Sunday School can last through the years. Young people who have shared in such activities as carol singing in hospitals or visiting Cheshire Homes have formed good and lasting friendships through serving others. While not excluding the possibility of enduring friendships outside the church, there is no doubt that the church is a good place to meet and make friends.

Being church members means accepting responsibilities. As children and young people we have been mostly on the receiving end of things, benefitting from the efforts, financial support and time that others have put into the life of the church. The time comes when we have to take our share of the responsibilities that others too may benefit. It is through our local church that we make our financial contribution to the upkeep of the church as well as for service and outreach. Some people expect the church to be there for the baptisms of their children, to provide a venue for their marriages and to arrange for their funerals when they die, but they never give a though to what it costs to maintain the buildings, to support the clergy, etc. There are many tasks to be done in maintaining the church and many of them are done by people who remain in the background, unnoticed by the majority of people who attend. Who is it that arranges the flowers week by week? Who repairs the altar cloths? Who oversees the gardens and provides that lovely display of flowers? Who comes early each week to open up the church for worship? These are few of the jobs people do which are taken for granted and go unrewarded. Unrewarded in one sense, but those who do them work for the love of the church and for Jesus and it is reward enough just to be able to serve.

'The' Church, 'My' church, or both? As we react in faith to the grace of God shown in Christ Jesus, and give witness of the fact through such steps as baptism or confirmation, we become part of The Church. But through the local congregation, which we can proudly and thankfully call 'My' church, we experience that membership in practical ways and take a full share in the family life of The Church.

Questions

1. "I regard all churches as the same, so I like to attend different ones for worship week by week." What, if anything, is wrong with this?

2. "My church is poor. We can hardly raise enough money to cover our own expenses, so we cannot give to outside causes or to missionary work." Why is giving to such causes right and how does a church benefit through giving to others?

3. "I often go to church, but I don't put much in the collection. The church is always asking for money and seems more interested in raising cash than preaching the gospel." Is this a valid reason for not giving, or just an excuse?

CHAPTER 4

What are my Gifts?

Have you ever entered a talent competition? Or perhaps you have heard someone referred to as 'a very talented musician'. Originally, the word 'talent' meant a coin, a piece of money with a specific value. When our Lord told the parable of the talents, He spoke of a different amount of money being given to three people to use for their master's service. You can read this story in Matthew 25: 14-30, and note the result for the servant who did not use the money entrusted to him. Today, the word 'talent' is more often associated with a special ability, often in the area of the arts, acting, singing, playing a musical instrument or perhaps painting

Not all talents, or gifts as we often call them, are so obvious or gain public acclaim. A good memory and ability to retain facts, mathematical skills and language skills may be talents that some seem to be born with, and you will be able to think of others that could be added to the list. And so we say that people have different gifts.

The use of the word 'gift' suggests that we mean something that is received quite freely and which becomes the possession of the receiver to use as he desires. If you were to be given a box of paints for a birthday present, you would not expect the donor to dictate to you exactly what pictures you are to paint with it. You will decide how to use this gift and, indeed, you may put it away in a cupboard and forget all about it, but this would certainly not show much appreciation for the gift, nor are you likely to develop an ability to paint. By making an attempt to paint a picture you will be both showing your appreciation for the gift and beginning to develop the ability to paint. There are indeed people who seem to have a natural ability to sing well, or act, or paint, etc., but if asked, each would say that for these abilities to reach their best, a lot of hard work has to go into developing and refining them.

Are all our talents gifts? Are we able to create talents for ourselves? Well, it has been said that anyone can sing well, if he/she is given the right training and is willing to put in the necessary effort. While not rising to heights of fame as singers, such people may well make a worthwhile contribution to the church choir. The proverb, 'Necessity is the mother of invention' may be expressed as 'A need produces a talent'. Some of us feel that we are quite untalented, but when we become aware of a need, perhaps in the church fellowship, possibly the need for Sunday School teachers, or someone to keep accounts, if we are willing to let God use us in these tasks, then we find that the necessary skill or talent can be learned and developed.

So we see that some talents are natural gifts and others can be developed in response to a need. All will need the discipline of practice and effort if they are to reach their full potential. How then, do we use our talents? We've already mentioned Sunday School teaching, singing in the choir, keeping accounts, etc., but does this mean that as Christians we regard 'talents' or 'gifts' as something only to be used within the life and structure of our church, and that the skills we use at other times as somehow different? No. Through the proper use of our God given and personally developed gifts, we can witness to the wholesomeness of the Christian life and serve our fellow men and women as surely as Christ would have us do. A thoroughly reliable accountant in a business firm is a great asset to that firm and when it is known that the reliable person is a Christian, then God's name is honoured.

Gifts, talents, skills, all have to be used, if they are to have any value. It is no good having a fine singing voice, practising daily and reaching a high standard of perfection, and then singing only in the shower! As Christians we need to identify our gifts, develop them through practice and then put them to good use. This 'good use' can be called 'the stewardship of skills and talents'.

How then, do we identify our talents? Some will be obvious such as singing. Some we may recognise with surprise. We have seen many young people who would have said that they had no acting ability who, having reluctantly accepted a part in a play, find that they not only have a gift for acting but also thoroughly enjoy it.

Sometimes it is someone else who sees the potential in you. Many have been led into successful careers through the advice of an older person who saw in them an ability that could be developed. Often a talent takes time to develop and one should not be put off by early failures. This may especially be true of Sunday School teaching or Lay preaching. It may be through trial and error that we find out what our gifts are. We may try something for a time and then dis-cover that we are not really suited to the task. There is nothing shameful about admitting this and going on to something else, pro-vided one has really put some effort into the task and made a sincere attempt to develop the skill.

So, having discovered, identified and developed our talents, what then? How do we use them? It surprises some young people when we talk about stewardship of talents. Stewardship of money—yes—but how can we be good stewards of our talents? Often people think of using their talents within the church structures only and that anything done outside the church in the secular world is of less value. Unfortunately there is a tendency among some to equate 'serv-ing God' to 'serving in a full-time church related job'. God does, of course, lead people into the ordained ministry or missionary work or some medical or education-related job, but every Christian should be in full-time service for God. Some indeed, have felt led to give up their secular job on becoming a Christian, which may be right for some, but more often God wants us to continue where we are and to serve Him there. For students this will mean honouring Him in our studies and gaining the best possible qualifications so that we may work in a realm where we can bring our Christian faith into the way we work. Cliff Richards was faced with this choice when he be-came a Christian—should he give up his singing career and find al-ternative 'full-time' service?. How glad we must be that he chose (or felt led) to continue as a singer, for surely he has been an inspi-ration to many young Christians who admire him. There are some but by no means enough Christians in the political sphere. We need Christian men and women in places where they can influence mat-ters that affect the lives of many people. The business world needs Christians. Teachers have a great deal of influence upon the lives of children and young people and through them, on their families. This doesn't mean that they will be preaching all the time–they would probably fail as teachers if they did–but their concern for their students and the way they try to help and be fair to all can make a great difference in the lives of the children. You will be able to think of other jobs in which Christians can be a blessing. Indeed, unless a job is blatantly evil, there is no profession that will not benefit from sincere Christian input.

Most of us must combine being actively Christian in our secular jobs and contributing our talents to the life of our local church community. This usually means giving time to serving in the church, time that we might consider to be our own. Just as all that we have materially belongs to God and we are stewards of it for Him, so our time and talents belong to Him. Of course, we need time for relaxation and leisure if we are to remain healthy. This is part of our good stewardship of our health. But all of us can give some time to helping in the life of the church. Again it is a matter of identifying our talents, being willing to develop new skills where necessary and being willing to serve alongside others, supporting and complementing each other as we bring our different skills and gifts into God's family.

Perhaps it is necessary to put in a word here about jealousy or envy. Sometimes we look at someone who seems to be so much more talented than we are and who, because of their particular gifts, receives much public acclaim, and we become envious. It doesn't seem fair. We may try to emulate their actions, trying to gain for ourselves some of the attention being given to them. There are two things wrong with this. Jealousy spoils relationships and also embitters the jealous person. It is never productive to good growth in the church fellowship. Secondly, while envying and trying to copy someone else, we fail to recognise and develop our own gifts. It may well be that the gifts we have will not bring us into the limelight. We may have to remain in the background as far as other people are concerned. But it is God whom we serve and not man. Whatever gift or talent He has given to us, He will also give opportunities to use in the work of His kingdom. It is from Him we want to hear the words, "Well done, good and faithful servant".

Questions

1. What is the difference between 'natural' talents and 'acquired' talents? Give an example of both.

2. Suggest ways in which our talents can be used both within the church structures and outside the church.

3. How can jealousy of another's talent spoil church fellowship? How can we avoid the problem of jealousy?

4. If this is a group study, let each suggest a talent or gift he/she recognises in the person sitting next to him/her and also name one talent in himself/herself.

5. Why is it necessary that each one's talents should be recognised and brought into the service of God's kingdom?

CHAPTER 5

Decisions

"What subjects shall I take at college?", "What shall I wear for the class reunion?", "Should I take the I.A.S. exam?", "Should I join a political Youth Group?", "Should I accept an invitation to join a trekking party?", "My parents want me to get married. Should I accept their choice of partner?", "I think God is calling me into the ministry. How can I be sure?", "Shall I cook chicken or fish tonight?". Decisions! Decisions! Life is full of decisions that have to be made. Some are life-shaping while others hardly seem to matter at all. But there is a sense in which all decisions, big or small, go into making us the sort of people that we are – or will become.

Does it matter whether we eat chicken or fish tonight? In one way, no, but behind the choice may lie another issue, one of family relationships. I may personally like fish but someone else in the family dislikes it. How do I show my love for each member of the family with individual likes and dislikes? What T.V. programme shall we watch tonight? Not a life-shattering decision you may say. But what does our choice reveal about our character, about our use of time, about our concern for others?

The bigger decisions that concern matters like our careers, our marriages, our political allegiances, may give us greater problems. It would seem that our future happiness, our health, our security, all depend on our making the right choices and, as Christian people, we realise that what we plan to do with our lives is bound up with finding what God's will is for us. How do we set about this?

Sometimes, when we are faced with the need to make an important decision, we may be told, "Make it a mattter of prayer." How glib this advice can sound. God doesn't usually speak from heaven and specify exactly what we are to do, does He? However, prayer does have an important part to play in helping us to come to correct decisions. In chapter two we were dealing with the topic of

a personal devotional life, and we thought of prayer being part of a
daily spiritual exercise. Daily prayer and Bible reading keeps our
spiritual compass set and helps us to walk in the right direction so
that when special decisions have to be made we already have some
idea of the direction we need to take.

Prayer keeps our consciences keen so that when we are faced
with some choices we will immediately recognise where the wrong
decision will lead. For example, that invitation to a trekking holiday
may help us fulfil a desire to visit a scenic part of the country that
we have always wanted to see. But we may also know something
about the characters of the group going and their habits. Perhaps
you suspect that experimenting with drugs or alcohol is going to be
part of the 'fun' of the expedition. Your conscience will be uneasy
about joining the group. The Holy Spirit causes us to feel uneasy
about things that are wrong and it is because we are maintaining
our daily time of communion with God that we are able to feel the
presence of the Holy Spirit in this way. We should always take a
feeling of unease seriously when we have to come to decisions .

Not all decisons involve a straight choice between right and
wrong, between good and evil, so it would seem that it is not always
possible for our consciences to come to our aid in making the right
choice. For example, deciding on a future career and therefore what
course of study or training we should take. The choice is wide and
there is no moral issue involved in choosing between medicine or
engineering, between teaching or business management, between
fashion modelling and nursing. This is an area in which the advice
and guidance of others may be helpful, but it has to be advice and
guidance, the final decision must be our own. In the previous chapter we were dealing with stewardship of talents and some of what
we said there is relevant here. Recognising our gifts and abilities is
essential and therefore we need to be honest with ourselves. We
would all like to be famous, 'stars' in some profession or other, but
we need to be honest and admit our lack of any necessary talent.
Unfortunately parents can sometimes bring undue pressure on their
children to undertake careers for which they have no real inclination or suitability. So, our first task is to be honest with ourselves
about our aptitudes and abilities and here together with parents, a

school career guidance officer or a teacher in whom we can trust may give us the best advice.

We also need to sort out what we are aiming for in pursuing any particular course of study or career plan. Are we aiming at making as much money as possible as quickly as we can? Or are we aiming at making the best possible use of intelligence, skills and opportunities that God gives us regardless of the financial implications? Money in itself is not evil and financial security is not to be ignored. Most of us are dependent upon our parents to finance us through college or training and we may have financial responsibilities toward our families as well as for ourselves and our future. It is not wrong to look for a proper reward for effort and input, but this will not be our first priority in deciding on a career.

Marriage is one of the most important decisions that we are likely to face. Unlike arranging a course of study which can be changed if it proves to be the wrong one for us, marriage is a life-long commitment. Where there are children, what we make of our marriage will affect their lives as well as ours. Is there any way in which we can be absolutely sure that we are making the right decision in such an important matter as well as in less serious concerns? We have a clue to the answer to this question in how we deal with less serious matters. The practice of seeking and accepting God's will for us in every area of life is good preparation for finding His will for us in these larger issues.

Let us go back to consider how we as Christians come to decisions. Firstly we maintain a discipline of daily communion with God through prayer and Bible study. (Bible study not just Bible reading. Taking time to study a few verses from the Bible to discover what it has to say, is of more value than reading a whole chapter at a time without giving much thought to its application.) This will keep us facing in the right direction and keep our consciences finely honed. Into this devotional time we will bring our specific requests. The answers may not be immediate, but we will find that gradually the rightness for us of one particular course of action rather than another will begin to impress itself upon us. This is the work of the Holy Spirit. Note that wherever possible we take time to consider matters and avoid snap decisions.

Sometimes we come to the right decision through a period of trial and error. An opportunity occurs, perhaps an offer of a job. We are not so sure whether or not we should take it. We make it a matter of prayer, but we do not seem to get any clear guidance about what we should do. We may seek advice from others and receive conflicting opinions. In such circumstances, and provided our consciences are quite clear about the nature of the job, it may be that we have to take the opportunity and do our best to make a success of it. God does give us the gift of 'commonsense' and there is every reason to suppose that He expects us to use it. If, after a fair period of trial and having put real effort into doing well, it becomes obvious that this is not the right place for us, then it may be best to look for something else and then resign. There may be nothing wrong with the job, but it may be the wrong job for us.

In none of our decisions can we act entirely as individuals seeking only what pleases ourselves. We are all part of a family and a community and what we do affects the lives of others. As Christians we have responsibilities; responsibilities towards our families and our communities. We have to consider others and the effect our decisions will have on them. Too often we think only of ourselves and what we want to do and give little thought to how the lives of others may be affected or influenced. So a third factor in coming to important decisions is, "How will this affect my family, my friends, my community?" It is also useful to consult other trusted, often senior, friends. Others who have your good at heart and also have much of life experience behind them, can give a mature Christian point of view. This is worth considering. It may be a bit irksome, because often we want to get on and do things in our own way, but God does use the Christian experience of others to help guide us, so it is up to us to allow Him the opportunity.

The biggest decision that most of us will have to face is probably that of marriage. In the first partnership recorded in the scripture, God gave Adam and Eve to each other. Through the centuries different marriage customs have developed in different cultures, but for Christians, whatever our cultural background, we believe that it is God who gives men and women to each other in marriage. However, unlike Adam and Eve, we do have a choice when it comes to this matter. Making the right choice is essential. In India the system of arranged marriages can be a great help in enabling young people with similar backgrounds to meet each other. Good parents will take the greatest care possible to ensure the suitability of the match. But the final decision is usually taken by the young people themselves. Like all important decisions, what has gone into the foundation of life from childhood upwards, i.e., loving care by parents, good examples in the lives of elders, sound moral teaching, careful living, will all have contributed to helping the young people come to the right decision now. How important it is for parents to realise that helping their children to make wise and proper decisions in life begins by the example and teaching given from their earliest years.

Sometimes it happens that young people fall in love with someone that their parents would not have chosen for them and tension arises within the family. One fact we have noted at such times is that the young people are usually very impatient and want to rush ahead and get married. Often they resent any suggestion that they should wait and are sure that their parents do not understand them. However, waiting is probably what is most necessary. Certainly all concerned must pray about it and allow time for God through His Holy Spirit to speak to them. He will probably remind them of the love their parents have for them and how it will take time for parents to understand and accept what is happening and to get to know the prospective partner. Those closely involved in such a problem may not want to hear this and may want to avoid praying, or they may try to demand that God makes the parents understand so that the young people can have their own way. It will be difficult to pray sincerely without being made aware of these other factors which some may prefer to ignore. And, if God does keep pressing the idea that waiting is an option, will it not be better to wait a year and hopefully start married life with the blessing and love of near and dear ones, rather than insist on an immediate decision suited to one side only and perhaps create a rift between children and parents that may never be healed? It is also possible that, although such waiting may seem restrictive and unnecessary, within that year God will either help all concerned to feel that the choice is acceptable or will lead away from that partnership and towards some other plan. In making this point, we presume that parents concerned will also take time for prayer and caring fellowship and not resort to intimidating pressure. All who are involved in such a problem need to wait upon God together. A readiness to wait and consider the feelings of parents may cause some disappointment, but it will also indicate a considerate attitude which itself will be a blessing within a life partnership.

The matter of dowry may also come into the picture. It is natural for parents to wish to see their children financially secure and to consider the earning capacity of the prospective partner, but when greed enters into the negotiations and demands for large sums of money or other material assets take precedence over the happiness of the young people, then a clash of will may ensue. As Christian young people it may well be necessary to make a definite stand against the matter of dowry even though it may lead to some strain in family relationships. To stand for a principle while at the same time showing love and consideration toward parents will be difficult, but God can use even such an experience to bless both children and parents.

Much of what has been said so far has been about personal and individual decisions. But all decisions cannot be made on this basis. Take, for instance, partners in business. One partner should avoid making a decision without the agreement of the other. Decisions need to be mutual. This is especially so in the marriage partnership. Matters such as a wife continuing in employment, how to manage finance, how to spend leisure time, when to start a family, the sharing of home duties and chores, continuing a close relationship with old friends, all need to be thought about and decided together.

How do we arrive at such mutual decisions? It may not be easy at first. Until marriage both partners have been in the habit of making decisions for themselves—and have been perfectly capable of doing so. After marriage there is a partner to consider and this can cause a certain sense of strain and frustration. But it is part of the adjustment that both partners have to learn to make. Earlier in this chapter the matter of praying together has been mentioned. It has to be mentioned again here. God intends unity in marriage, and for both partners to pray to God as a unit helps both partners to sense God's will. Open and frank discussion between the partners is needed, as also is the readiness on both sides to listen to the other partner. So often the dominant partner does not want to listen to the other and can be angry or sulk when they do not get their own way. Face such a danger together and avoid it by taking time to discuss matters coolly. If conversation gets overheated, postpone the discussion. In a moment's anger a lot of hurtful things can be said, and they are hard to undo. Avoid resentment building up when there seems to be a lack of understanding, and avoid tit-for-tat remarks. Resentment has a corroding effect on relationships. A little good humour and laughter at such times helps a lot. Some questions we have to face take time and effort to answer. Partners need to work at such problems, trying to do what is best for the partnership and not attempting merely to impose one point of view. Mutual trust in business and family relationships is essential and care should be taken never to allow that trust to be undermined.

Questions

1. In what way does a discipline of daily devotions help us to make good decisions?

2. Is the advice of older people a help or a hindrance to us in learning to take decisions for ourselves?

3. 'I want to be a model, my parents want me to be a doctor and my school careers adviser suggest that I would make a good teacher.' How do I resolve this dilemma?

4. 'I feel that God wants me to be a missionary, but my parents have made great sacrifices to pay for my education. They are now getting old and will be looking to me to support them.' How can I be sure that I am making the right decision?

5. Does the Bible have any relevance to the decisions we have to make in our modern society?

CHAPTER 6

Relationships

The gospel is about relationships, first our relationship to God and then our relationship to our fellow men. We express our relationship to God in the way we relate to other people. Our experience tells us that we affect and are affected by the people we live with, those we choose as our friends and the people we work alongside in our daily occupations. It has been said that our relationship to God affects our relationship to people and our relationship to people affects our relationship to God. Being in a right relationship with God enables us to cope with the pressures put upon us by our relationships with others. Good, healthy relationships, free from guilty feelings, with family, friends and colleagues help us to maintain our fellowship with God.

When we join the church as full members, each has to make his own respnse to the Bishop's question. There may be a group of people all being received into membership at the same time but the fact remains that each is responsible for the response made. No one can make a promise or commitment for someone else.

As we continue along the Christian way, we continue to be accountable for our own attitudes and actions. We do many things in the company of others, but nevertheless are responsible to God as individuals for our good deeds and our sins. However, we can never live as isolated beings. There have been people who have chosen to live solitary lives as hermits, but even they are usually dependent upon others for their food. Most of us live in definite relationships with other people. There will be our families both immediate and extended. We will begin to relate to a wider circle of people when we start school and begin to form our first friendships. Later there will be college friends and colleagues in the work-place. There will be those with authority over us and others over whom we have some degree of oversight. As Christian people, we have to learn how to relate to all these. Some of these relationships will be ones that we have chosen for ourselves–our friends, for example. Others, our families, those we work alongside, are not of our own choice. Some we will have very close association with. Others less. Some we find it easy to get along with. Others we do not find compatible and have to make a real effort to get on with. It is often in the field of relationships that our Christian discipleship is most tested.

The two areas in which we probably find our best and our worst relationships are our families and our church fellowship. Both can offer us the support and security we need, but both can present situations where we clash with others.

Let us take the family first. Born into this world as helpless babies, we begin life absolutely dependent upon others to provide the nourishment and protection we need to survive–usually our parents. Our first words are usually 'Mama' and 'Papa', and when we hurt ourselves as toddlers, we cry for Mummy or Daddy to heal the hurt. Quite early in life, usually as a toddler, a child begins to test his independence. When Mummy says "Don't touch", the child decides to touch the forbidden object to see what the result will be! Soon the child learns that there are good reasons why parents issue instructions and learns that obedience brings rewards and disobedience brings punishment or at least a feeling of the parents' displeasure. But as children grow older, new interests come into their lives, new hobbies, new friends. Some of the rulings given by parents no longer seem to be reasonable or justified. Clashes develop and, sadly, if not handled properly, the loving, trusting relationship between parent and child begins to be spoiled. However, this growing independence of thought and action is part of the normal process of growing up and should lead to developing maturity and a proper sense of responsibility. A child who does not learn to handle his own independence properly within relations in the home and is always adamant in getting his own way, or is totally submissive to the will of others, will fail to develop his full potential in life.

Christian young people will face this dilemma just as much as others but because they wish to please Christ in all things, they will endeavour to resolve difficulties harmoniously. It needs to be emphasised both to parents and to those who expect to become parents some day, that great care needs to be taken to foster good parent/ child relationships from the earliest years of the child and right through to adulthood. There can be no greater satisfaction for parents than to see their children develop into caring independent adults who retain the love and respect for their family.

How then do we tackle these clashes when they arise? Perhaps the first essential is to develop the habit of communication. Keeping our parents in the dark about what we are doing or what we plan to do contributes to misunderstandings. Sometimes we make plans concerning which we have no communication with our parents and resent it when they do not immediately agree. For example, imagine a group of young people who form the idea that they would like to make a trip to the Valley of Flowers. As they talk about it among themselves, they begin to get very excited about the prospect. One will obtain brochures about the area. Another will find out details about travel and cost. Another may plan what food they will need to take and so on. None of this is shared with their parents. At last, shortly before the trip is to take place, one, who now feels somewhat embarrassed to put the idea forward, suddenly confronts the parents with a demand for the money to cover the cost and the fact that "We are going!" Is it surprising that the parents' immediate response is negative? An argument will probably follow, parents pointing out the dangers as they see them, questioning who is to be in the party; the young person responding with "You don't trust me!" All the ingredients are there for a big family row. How different it might have been if the idea had been shared with the parents from the beginning. Instead of the embarrassment of having to face friends with the answer that "My parents won't let me come", there might have been joint discussions with parents who could have given advice and been able to agree on a trip that they knew to have been well planned with safeguards against emergencies built in. Many clashes can be avoided if we take time to talk. Losing our temper or sulking will never resolve a problem. Talking things through helps us to understand each other's point of view.

The principle of good communication leading to good relationships is appplicable in areas other than family life. There are many reasons why relationships in a church fellowship sometimes break down and poor coomunication is often one of them. Where people are ill-informed, rumours which may be quite untrue gain acceptability. One way to build and maintain good relationships in a church fellowship is to make sure that we ascertain the true facts about situations that arise. This may be difficult as people with their own axe to grind will be anxious to relate the facts as they support their own standpoint. Listening to and acting upon untruths or half-truths leads to misunderstanding and division, so one must always be careful to sort out truth from rumour.

In striving to build up good relationships within a church fellowship, we will be helping others who share the same concern. At the beginning of the chapter we said how we affect and are affected by others. When we are making an effort to encourage good relationships in a church or in any other group of people, we will find that there are others who feel as we do and we are able to strengthen and encourage one another. However, we must be careful not to form an exclusive group of people whose efforts are marred by a sense of self-righteousness, a 'holier than thou' sort of attitude. Remember that our aim is good fellowship with all as far as this is possible.

A good way to avoid bad relationships and build good ones is to be engaged in positive actions. It is said that the devil finds work for idle hands to do and he certainly finds opportunities to do his work among idle Christians. Working together to produce a play or a concert in aid of some good cause will give people a shared sense of purpose. The interaction of working together helps us to get to know and understand each other. The shared satisfaction of doing something worthwhile draws people together. There are many openings for such joint action. Organising an outing for deprived children, running coaching classes at exam time for poorer students are just a couple of suggestions. Working together in this way means that there will be neither the time nor the inclination for quarrelling.

Cliquishness is another cause of poor relationships. We all have a tendency to gravitate towards the people we like, those who speak the same mother tongue as we do, those who have the same educational background as we have, and we become so satisfied within our own little groups that we make no effort to cross boundaries and get to know other people. We impoverish our lives by not experiencing the enrichment of fellowship we can have with a wider variety of people. The tendency to form small cliques within a church also leads to misunderstandings and disputes. Each clique claims the right to have things done their way. They have no understanding, nor wish to have, of the traditions and inclinations of others. A mutual contributing and blending of traditions and ideas enhances and enriches the worship and fellowship of a church. We are the losers when we deny others the right to share their experiences with us. It takes an effort of will to move from the safety of the familiar into the adventure of building new relationships, but it is well worth making that effort.

Another help in creating and maintaining good relationships both in the home and elsewhere, is the practice of thinking oneself into the situation of other people. Most animals are, by nature, selfish and we seem to share this tendency with them. We like to please ourselves, satisfy our own needs and desires with little thought about how our own satisfaction will affect the lives of others. Within a family we have to learn to share, but we may still take much of what is given and done for us selfishly. Occasionally thinking ourselves into say, our mother's situation, of how tired she must get preparing food day after day, trying to keep the home attractive for us and for our friends who come, may make us a little more appreciative and willing to help with some of the chores. Thinking ourselves into the situation of a brother who is studying hard for an important examination, may help us to be more tolerant of his irritability and understanding of his need for more quiet and less music being played. Many clashes within a church fellowship can be avoided by making the effort to see things from another's point of view and taking time to allow the other person to explain why he feels as he does–and really listening to what he says! Being willing to listen to another will help him to be willing to listen to you.

Relationships are spoiled by obstinacy and being unwilling ever to admit that we may be wrong and to apologise. Disagreements grow and spread, their roots go down deep and ill-feeling between rivals can become so entrenched that there seems to be almost no hope of restoring harmony, and all because no one wanted to admit to an error! Paul in his letter to the Romans (12:18) says, "If possible, so far as it depends upon you, live peaceably with all." This is a challenge for every young Christian not only to strive for good relationships between oneself and others but also to act as peacemaker within the church fellowship. Although this may at first seem an impossible task for young Christians, yet, going a step at a time, God can use you. Refuse to be drawn into other people's arguments, but rather show friendship to all. Try to help people see each other's point of view.

Maintaining good relationships with those in authority over us may appear to be outside our control. Here keeping the lines of communication open doesn't seem to depend on us. The opportunity for open and free discussion of problems may not be given to us. But we can do a lot to foster good and harmonious relationships even in this sphere. First a proper respect for the position and authority of our 'bosses'. Paul says, "Pay respect to whom respect is due" (Romans 13:7) and this applies to our employers as well as to those in government. A careful and disciplined attitude to work and time-keeping, gives the 'boss' no cause for complaint. A cheerful readiness to put in extra effort when necessary and a loyalty to the well being of the firm, will all help. The Christian can offer no excuse for careless work, for unpunctuality or time-wasting and cannot expect his boss to excuse such behaviour. However, there may be times when, despite our best efforts, the people under whom we work impose unreasonable and unbearable burdens upon us and we do have to confront them. This should be done after prayer for the guidance of the Holy Spirit and making every effort to speak calmly, taking care not to allow loss of temper or a rude way of speaking to rob us of our clarity of purpose.

Questions

1. In what ways can the relationships we form with people affect our relationship to God?

2 What is the role of parents in establishing and maintaining good family relationships?

3. "Many of my colleagues at work are involved in practices of which I, as a Christian, disapprove. How can I maintain my own principles and yet remain in good relationship with my colleagues?

4. Paul says "As far as possible, live in peace with everyone." (Romans 12:18). How far is it "possible"? Are there times when we cannot live in peace? If so, in what circumstances?

5. Some of the great men and women of history have not been easy people to get on with. Why? Discuss.

CHAPTER 7

Male and Female He created Them

In the previous chapter we thought about relationships. Now we turn our attention to one of the most important relationships known to society, the relationship of marriage. We shall also touch on the matter of sex, because, although marriage means much more than deep sexual relationship, we believe marriage is the correct context for it.

What is the ideal marriage? What would you want out of marriage? It is worthwhile, even if you are already married, spending time to make a list for yourself of aspects of an ideal marriage. The following are a few examples of what may come to mind. You may easily add a number of other items to the list.

* Marriage is a Partnership. In this
* Partners are different but complement and assist each other;
* Plans can be made for a 'life-long' relationship;
* There is absolute loyalty to each other, the partners being able to trust each other at all times, whether they are together or one is absent;
* There is openness. No secrets are kept from each other;
* Neither partner purposely makes the other feel unworthy or criticises in company;
* Thoughts, plans, efforts are shared;
* Neither partner is wasteful, nor too stingy;
* Sympathy and respect for the other partner is shown;
* A loyal, loving and thoughtful relationship is maintained, for you can put up with a lot of difficulty or poverty when you have a supportive partner;
* Failures can be admittted, forgiven and forgotten.

All these aspects require working at. They do not necessarily come naturally or easily. A mango tree does not grow, flower and fruit in one day, or even in one year. If you have a 'best friend', just consider how long it has taken for the friendship to develop. Understanding such a friend has taken months and years. Probably incidents such as holidays, dangers, hurdles, common likes and dislikes have helped the friendship to grow. Most of us keep quiet about our innermost thoughts and desires, but we may share such things with our best friend. One's marriage partner should be the very best friend of all, but such friendship takes time to grow. Gradually we get to know the other person and secrets can be shared. Sometimes we do not like all that we discover. Even when we consider ourselves we find aspects of our characters which we do not like and of which we are not proud. Some of us are hard to live with and some of us do not fully understand ourselves. Let us recognise that one of the benefits of a reasonably long engagement, say six to twelve months, is that we can get to know the other person to some extent before we make the life-long commitment of marriage.

The above paragraph can be read in three minutes, but it takes much longer to take on board its meaning. A garden or a field will not look after itself automatically. There has to be sowing, nourishing, pruning, maintenance. Only then can we hope for a reasonable harvest; –and weeds constantly grow uninvited. Similarly, marriage will not look after itself automatically.

Don't let this daunt you. Marriage is an adventure. It is exciting, enjoyable, rewarding, but it also involves a loyalty and interdependence which calls for discipline and appreciation. Thanking a partner for a job well done or a meal nicely cooked, remembering a birthday or avoiding words or habits that irritate, is all part of the picture.

In such circumstances what happens to our personal independence, our skills, likes and dislikes? Does our individuality have to be squashed and denied in order to give way to our partner? Basically the answer is 'No'. Sometimes our more selfish attitudes have to be modified by a real act of willpower, but such gradual changes go along with a development of personality. In each one of us there is our personal 'ego' which is essential because without it we would be robots. But the ego does change as we go through life, and true love can help the ego change for the better. As each partner in a marriage aims to work for the other's good, a mutual adaptation is taking place.

It is in this growing, developing relationship of complete commitment in marriage that sexual intercourse is enjoyed. The act is so personal, expressive, and at its best so satisfying, that it belongs to the unity of a life-long relationship. It is part of the wholesome process of getting to know each other. It needs to be said that complete melting together is not necessarily achieved on one's honeymoon. Great and lovely expectations are OK, but they may not be realised immediately. A loving partner is an understanding partner, so even frustration and disappointment can be coped with in marriage. Gradually the sex act comes to express the complete unity, love and confidence that a husband and wife can have for each other.

As Christian people, is there any guidance that we can get from the Bible? The following passages give us something to think about.

In Genesis 2 God gives Eve to Adam as a helper and partner. It is a one-to-one relationship and is set up to provide companionship and to fulfil God's good purpose. Both partners are capable of talking with God and are given the chance to fulfil something of God's design. This partnership also provides the opportunity to disobey God together and both suffer together on this account.

The last chapter of Proverbs 31, from verse 10 onwards describes an ideal wife and mother. We could hope there would be an equally demanding description of an ideal husband! But what we do see is the woman's skill in ordering her own household is recognised and we note she has her own bank account and freedom to start up a business. Her husband is well spoken of because of her ability and he appreciates this help and says so to her.

Ephesians 5: 21-33, stresses an equality in relationship and we note that this equality is interactive between the partners. It does not concern itself with how others look at the two partners, but how the partners develop their relationship between themselves. "Be subject to one another" says a lot to every husband and wife about listening to the other, appreciating the other, giving honour to the other, a *pahile aap* sort of courtesy, and a saying "sorry" when mistakes are made (which implies an acceptance of such an apology also!).

The apostle Peter has his own contribution to make in 1 Peter 3: 1-7.

In Mark 10: 2-12, where the Pharisees are questioning Jesus about divorce, probably with the idea of finding fault with him on some legal point, He makes an interesting comment about "the two becoming one", an indication that in the sight of God and in accord with His design, the two partners in a marriage form a unit. This unit is not intended again for sub-division. If we see an apple tree in fruit, and one of the fruits should be hanging there cut in half, would we regard that half as useful and marketable?

Paul in 1 Corinthians 7 makes some interesting deductions about this 'Unit' of a married couple and about the regard and obligations each should have for the other.

The unit formed by two persons in marriage is easily forgotten when pressures come along, and part of that pressure comes from the lifestyle of society in general. Because non-Christian society treats marriage as a legal contract which can be impermanent, why not Christians also? We are not dismissing the pressures and sometimes the agony that face some people in marriage. Such pressures are real and deep, and the causes need to be recognised wherever possible and faced up to. And the strength to face them comes out of the gospel itself.

It is obvious from passages in scripture, some of which are quoted above, that sexual temptations are as common among Christians as anyone else. The important thing is to recognise that such urges have to be kept under control. There is a right place for sex, which we have indicated is within marriage and also within a truly loving relationship, but we recognise there is plenty of opportunity for immorality, especially in a society where contraception appears to grant the freedom to have sex without having babies.

Our view is that humans are not made on the level of animals that want to mate whenever and wherever the urge comes, but as beings with a God-given sense of responsibility, honour, sacrificial love and self-control. Experience of true love is not in promiscuous sex, but in properly controlled love within a lasting partnership, and that sort of love has the blessing of God on it.

Having said so much about partnership, what is to be said to the person for whom marriage never seems to come along? Some who greatly desire marriage never succeed in finding the proper partner. To such persons, with love and sympathy we would say, please realise that marriage is not the only key to happiness and success. The single person can exploit certain advantages–a freedom to attain status, undertake jobs and travel–that are not open to many who are married. Good healthy friendships can help a lot. Always be wary of unscrupulous persons who are basically wanting to take unfair advantage of lonely people, but a good friendship or group of friends can be a real help in providing mutual support, especially as age increases.

A word needs to be said about homosexuality. To have a good trusted friend of the same sex is natural and right. However, to use such a relationship to stimulate and give vent to the urge to 'have sex' together is unnatural and unhealthy. Just as sodomy and fornication is condemned in the Old Testament, so it is also ruled out in the New. When we read such passages as Romans 1: 26-27, "women exchanged natural relations for unnatural, and the men likewise gave up natural relations with women and were consumed with passion for one another, men committing shameless acts with men and receiving in their own persons the due penalty for their error," we realise there is nothing new or novel about such activities. It is quite possible that the urge and opportunity to work up such a relationship may occur in quite a low key way without any premeditation. It may seem quite 'natural' and harmless but we need to take note of what the word of God says. If it puts such a relationship out of bounds and views it as sinful, it will be well for us to take this line also. Usually we discover that the laws of God are not invented by God to stop us from having a good time, but are given as guidelines to help humankind get the best out of life. These 'laws' have stood the test of time and are for the benefit of people and show proper respect for persons and society. Yet there remains the dilemma of a person who is born with homosexual inclinations. Are we to condemn such a man or woman as a sinner to be shunned or as a reprobate for whom there is no hope of God's saving grace in Christ? Here we must tread with care. People who are born with unusual physical features cannot be written off spiritually, so it seems wise to apply the same attitude to those with homosexual orientation. But what would we advise them about expressing their sexuality? Realising this may sound hard to such a person, we would nevertheless counsel, "If the Bible rules it out, then, as all the rest of us have to do, ask God for help to deny yourself and act according to the scriptures".

We conclude with a warning about self-righteousness. None of us is perfect and we need to be constantly and humbly aware of this. Yet where we realise an act is wrong, where scripture says it is wrong, we have to admit the fact and avoid it ourselves and advise others against such habits. Once again we come round to the problem, how to love the sinner while recognising the sin? It is not easy to keep the balance, but this is what we have to do.

Questions

1. The marriage partnership has responsibilities on both sides. What are some of these responsibilities? In the Indian context specially think about relationships with the in-laws.

2. What helps love grow in marriage?

3. Does marriage get in the way of a career?

4. How can the church improve its care of single people?

5. What should the church do about homosexual tendencies?

CHAPTER 8

Everybody Does it - Why Don't I?

This is a chapter about do's and don'ts, about why followers of Christ do some things and don't do others. It is basic for us to try to follow Jesus as a pattern of manhood, an example of what human beings are meant to be. We cannot see God who is Spirit, but Jesus brings God into focus, so when we see what Jesus did and didn't do we have some guidelines to show us how His followers should act.

Jesus had a wholesome respect for the Law which God had given to Israel through Moses. For instance, Jesus said, "It is easier for heaven and earth to pass away than for one dot of the law to become void" (Luke 16:17) or, in the Sermon on the Mount, "Do not think that I have come to abolish the law and the prophets... I have come to fulfil them. Until heaven and earth pass away, not an iota, not a dot, will pass from the law until all is accomplished. He who does them and teaches them shall be called great in the Kingdom of Heaven." Jesus was Himself a great Teacher. In the gospels He is often reported as *teaching*, but regarding the Teachers of the Law, the Scribes and Pharisees, he advised, "(they) sit on Moses' seat; so practice and observe whatever they tell you, but not what they do; for they preach, but do not practice." In some instances like Matthew 6:11, He specifically warned against the teaching of the Pharisees and Sadducees. In the Sermon on the Mount He went on to say (Matt. 5:20), "Unless your righteousness exceeds that of the Scribes and Pharisees, you will never enter the Kingdom of heaven."

When asked to identify the greatest commandment, Jesus did not pick one of the Ten Commandments, but referred to the passage in Deuteronomy 6: 4 & 5, the 'Shema', which was most important for all Jews, "You shall love the Lord your God with all your heart and with all your soul and with all your mind (see Matt. 22:36f) and quickly followed on with the counterpart in Leviticus 19:18, "And the second is like it, you shall love your neighbour as yourself," and added, "On these two commandments depend all the law and the prophets."

As those who seek to follow Jesus, we have to be tough on ourselves and keep in line with our Saviour's teaching. Otherwise we are really saying, "Thanks, I need your blessing, but I'm not prepared to follow your teaching", which, if we are honest with ourselves, provides a grand example of the stubborness of sin!

Many of us, perhaps most of us, live in a democratic country. We have the freedom to choose our representatives in local and national government and we enjoy a great sense of freedom in expressing our own ideas, likes and dislikes. We should be thankful for those who have won this freedom for us. However, in every mode of government there is a danger. Democracy can be misleading when it infers that an action is right if the majority of people favour it. Most people who travel by railway would appreciate free travel, but obviously ticketless travel will not pay for the transport service we enjoy (or don't enjoy sometimes!). Doing the right thing is NOT guaranteed by a show of hands. In fact, so often it is the minority that has to challenge the wrongness of a majority decision. Prophets have often been single figures who have had to point out disobediences of the masses in the sight of God. When Pilate asked the mob what he should do with Jesus who was blameless, they shouted back, "Crucify him", and we know that Pilate gave way to the clamour of the seeming majority. How misleading the masses can be.

Let us recap on what we have thought about so far. Christians believe in Law so long as it is godly. They also believe that respect for God and care and consideration for fellow human beings is the basis for correct action. They have to be beware of accepting that any action is right just because the shout of the majority tells them 'This is OK'.

Now let us apply this to things around us starting with physical fitness. Is it a good thing to be physically fit? –'Yes'. Is it a good thing to help others to be physically fit? –'Yes'. Is it a good thing to eat well in order to keep physically fit? –'Yes'. Is it a good thing to be always munching and crunching, stocking up with calories and carbohydrates? –'Hold on. Don't go so fast!' What do we find in this simple illustration? Surely we find that it is possible to have too much of a good thing. Good food unbalanced by good exercise is no longer a good thing! It can become a positively bad thing in that it can invite a heart attack. But too much exercise under the wrong conditions can also lead to a heart attack. Athletes in training for some achievement will discipline themselves and keep up the pressure on muscle, diet, routine, and it will be wholesome for them. But many non-athletes could not keep up such a pace and would not be well-advised to attempt it. So, caring for physical fitness is part of 'loving oneself', and part of caring for others. There is a need for balance in all this. A need for wisdom and a need to recognise that there is a great variation amongst people. Not all of us will benefit from the same diet or from extreme forms of exercise.

In the last paragraph but one we used the phrase 'respect for God and care and consideration for fellow human beings'. We could have used the word 'love', saying 'love for God and love for our fellows', but did not do so because 'love' has such a range of meanings that it does not always convey the best. The best sort of love, such as the meaning of the verse where Jesus asked Peter, 'Do you love me?', is the love which is willing to be faithful and to make sacrifices for the sake of the other person. We mention this because when we speak of 'loving ourselves' (as e.g. when Jesus said, "You shall love your neighbour as yourself") we are not considering a sloppy love that indulges every whim and fancy, but a disciplined care that sets itself to do the very best even though it means enduring discomfort.

Many people enjoy wearing the latest fashion. If the fashion is long sleeves, everybody wants long sleeves. If the 'in' thing is to dress casually, then everything must be casual. You know the sort of thing we mean. If you fit into the pattern of the crowd, you feel comfortable. If you are dressed awkwardly or 'out of fashion' you hate being seen! It is a common experience. It is also a costly experience. We realise that often fashion designers are setting new trends in order to boost sales. To be trendy means we must be spendy. A successful fashion line can truly line the pockets of garment manufacturers.

It is a bit hard when some with a seemingly unlimited store of cash turn up time and again with new outfits, while many others just have to make do with what they have and probably feel rather shy about it. The trend may not only be in clothes. It may extend to apparatus like CD players and discs, or jewellery, or smoking or TV's or cars, etc., etc.

What should a Christian do about 'fashion'? We suggest that

1.   It is not being necessarily Christian to be old fashioned.

2.   It is not being necessarily Christian to go for every new fashion that comes out.

3.   A sound judgement is needed that can decide, 'I can spend .... on clothes every quarter, and it must stop there. To spend money like water is helping no one except the manufacturers.

4.   It is worthwhile reflecting on the fact that some people in this world are so poor that their concern is not 'Can I have the latest fashion?' but 'Can I get any new clothes at all?' The same goes for food and diet, for education, for leisure activities and entertainment. A Christian knows that it is right to limit one's own spending in a desire to benefit someone else. To build up a wardrobe full of saris is possible, but to think of the millions who cannot afford such choice and restrict one's own choice with the poor in mind is showing response to a nudge from God.

5.   One other aspect of 'fashion' needs to be noted. There are fashions which are designed to so emphasise the human figure, especially the female figure, that the result is come-hitherish and sexy. So be alert not to sacrifice your naturally demure style on the altar of fashion.

Doing what is 'socially acceptable' touches every aspect of life. In order to be 'in' with your own group you may be inclined to do the modern thing. We have to ask whether the 'socially acceptable' thing is acceptable from a Christian standpoint also. Things such as smoking, drinking, drug taking and promiscuous sex are all part of the scene, so be warned and be thoughtful.

Smoking is a habit that many experiment with. It looks big. It gives an air of nonchalant ease with the world and it also gives you something to do. Consequently, it can bring with it a certain stability, relaxation of nervous tension, peace of mind and enjoyment. But like most habits it has its 'down' side. Medical research tells us that those who smoke are at greater risk of getting lung cancer. People who do not like cigarette smoke being puffed in their faces object to being forced to be 'passive smokers'. It can become addictive. The person who now smokes five packets a day, sometime long ago started with one packet every three days. For some it is a smelly habit and, not the least, it costs money which could be spent on wholesome nourishment.

Although some of us live in a society where it is not unacceptable to smoke, we need to consider what effect our actions have upon other people. If you visit Nepal, you will find many in the church who gave up smoking when they became Christians because it represents the 'old' *biradari,* smoking being one of a cluster of sleazy habits such as gambling, drinking, foul language, dirty jokes, –do we need to extend the list? Personally, we would prefer to live in a smoke-free zone. People who go to Nepal to work with the church need to give up smoking out of respect for the people of the country rather than carry on smoking and expect the Nepalis to appreciate you liberal upbringing. They would not see it that way.

These days drugs, glue sniffing, and the like are on school and college campuses and provide a 'high' opt out from the pressures and responsibilities, unhappiness and loneliness of the learn/test education/examination routine. Such opportunities present themselves. It is interesting that those who have themselves become hooked take a delight in getting other people hooked also. Friends will tell you that you can try out these substances and see for yourself whether they give you a lift or not. "If you don't like them, you can leave them!" is part of the persuasive but badly flawed patter. Our answer to this problem is most clearly made by taking a look at people who have got hooked. Most of us have at least passing acquaintance with people whose minds have been blown, whose health has been undermined and whose ability to concentrate has been destroyed beyond repair. How would you like to finish up your youth by getting totally wrecked? Most of us would run a mile! That then is what to do. Avoid it like the plague.

The use of alcohol is another temptation for young people. Is it a sin to have a glass of wine? Let's face it. When Jesus was on earth many Jewish people used to drink a glass of wine at the sabbath meal or at wedding celebrations, and who can say whether the cup of wine which Jesus blessed was fermented or unfermented? But there's a lot of difference between a glass of wine for your health's sake and a bottle of gin to induce a stagger. We can never imagine Jesus allowing the balance of his own senses to go out of control. We note His refusal to accept wine before the crucifixion. If wine had got at Him, He might have given way and avoided the horror of the cross! There is no doubt that one effect that alcohol has is to blur the mind and dull the senses. Long before this, when Lemuel was receiving instruction on how to be a good leader he was told,

> it is not for kings to drink wine, or for rulers to desire strong drink; lest they drink and forget what has been decreed, and pervert the rights of all the afflicted. (Proverbs 31:4)

There's good sound reason for the slogan: 'Don't drink and drive'. Bear in mind a couple of things that the Apostle said. In 1 Corinthians 5:11, Corinth being a cosmopolitan and commercial seaport with plenty of vice around, he advised, "Don't associate with idolaters, drunkards or robbers." To Christians at Ephesus, another big city but in Asia, he says, "Do not get drunk with wine for that is debauchery, but be filled with the Spirit." So make sure the Holy Spirit is in charge of your life and He will help you to deal with these problems when they come.

While you may well have been instructed on the matter of money elsewhere, it is well to note that it can be a curse or a blessing. There is nothing wrong in earning money and building up your savings, but it is easy for cash and possessions to become an overriding obsession. Honesty, personal credibility, faithfulness and Christian fellowship can all be thrown to the winds in pursuit of money or possessions. While it is true that it is nice to have a reliable income and some money in the bank, it is also true to say that money of itself cannot guarantee happiness. By all means work for your wages, but regard the cash as something given to you 'on trust' for a while. Use it for the needs of your family and yourself, etc., but put aside a portion as "God's tenth" and from this tenth give to God's work in your local church as well as God's work in direct ways where you can help your fellow human beings.

But beware of beggars. Not because they are unworthy of your attention, but because you do not know where their money goes. If a person is hungry, provide something to eat. If a person needs help, try to provide a little job from which they can earn something. One of the best gifts you can give them is to help them realise that you treat them as your fellow human beings, that they are not worthless and that they are worth something to God. One of the tremendous examples Jesus gave us by living among us was that God is interested in people. Every person is of value in God's sight, so in the name of Jesus we treat people as people. It is true that beggars can be quick to spot a 'softie', can spin a plausible story and can take advantage of your kindness. Never mind! Be on your guard, by all means, but look them in the eyes and, even if you are not in a position to help them, give them a kind word not a curse.

Approaching Delhi by train one day, our compartment was invaded by commuters from Ghaziabad some of whom quickly settled down to a game of cards. We were fascinated by the amount of money being wagered on each deal. It could have been a week's wage packet won or lost, and neither winner nor loser wanted to stop betting. The ease with which Rs. 5/- and Rs. 10/- notes were changing hands was intriguing and caused us to wonder at such an apparent casual attitude to money. But that is what betting does. It is exciting (except, we suppose, when you're enduring a losing streak) and seems to add a chemical to the bloodstream so that each person remains mesmerised by the fascination of a flutter. Probably not one of the minor gamblers we were looking at would admit to being much poorer on account of the morning's losses, but we did wonder whether the wives or mothers of those concerned would happily see their week's housekeeping money whisked away into someone else's pocket by the turn of a greasy card. But that's the thing about gambling, like may questionable issues, it generates it own feverish addiction and before long, out of a hundred such persons, a certain percentage will be hooked—and a certain percentage ruined!

There we have it! What's wrong with a harmless raffle? One of the best arguments we have heard put forward by a fellow Christian was to the effect that Re. 1/- ticket hurts no one yet gives equal opportunity for anyone to win a prize. It is very difficult to counter that sensible view. Yet when we know the family's bread winner who will blow most of a month's salary on a lottery ticket that might make 'this poor man' rich, and when we know of artisans who, day after day, cannot bring themselves to go off for a day's work because they want to see the result of the lottery draw at noon which may net them the equivalent of a whole month's wages—but never does! —don't we feel that the basis of our optimism is a bit shaky? Go one step more and visit the hutments occupied by the unfortunate families, who because of one member's unwise flutters are forced to forego what little bit of nourishment they need, or clothing, or education, who get beaten because they complain, who get exploited because they exist in grinding poverty and who may be sold by an unloving parent to get money to satisfy his or her uncontrollable addiction, and the positive evil becomes a little clearer. Probably we should feel happier about this, if we could guarantee that everyone had a strong will and that out of Rs. 500/- no man would give more than Rs. 1/- to a raffle, or that everyone would sometimes get some worthwhile prize. But that isn't the way life works, and it doesn't provide the excitement of a gamble.

Just as there are societies such as Alcoholics Anonymous that try to help those caught in the tentacles of strong drink, so there are groups to help compulsive smokers and gamblers. It would probably surprise us to know the inside story of some of those being helped. We would find lives that are full of suffering, quarrelling, marriages at risk or families that have broken up, loneliness, ill-health and guilt, and the reason for such a sorry state of affairs is that somewhere, sometime, these folk bought their first drink or chose their first ticket. "Too bad!" you may say; "These people were not strong willed enough." And you would be right. The trouble is that no one knows his own strength of will, or his innate weakness, until the testing time comes. But, of one thing we can be quite sure, the person who refuses a drink the first time it is offered will be more able to refuse the second time, and the third, and so on. Sometimes on holiday we go to places where the edge of a cliff is unsafe and crumbling. We feel it right and sensible to tell our children 'Keep away from the edge' and to do the same thing ourselves. Would you walk on such an unsafe edge so that you could test it for yourself?

It is like that with gambling. Have a look at the money you have earned. God's given you the health and strength and opportunity to work for it. The money is now 'yours', so will it be right to spend Rs. 5/- on a lottery ticket, or will you feel (reluctantly, perhaps) that it will be better to decide 'I will spend that Rs. 5/- where I know it will do some good'? Personally we feel it better and right to put our money and our strength and our time where we feel it is going to be of use to God, and if, on reading that, you feel it to be 'a counsel of perfection', a weakness rather than strength, then you have to make that choice, but don't forget Perfection is something we mentioned earlier because Jesus mentioned it when He said, "Be perfect, therefore, as your heavenly Father is perfect." (Matthew 5:48).

This all sounds very fine as we share our thoughts with you, but one further thing has to be said. It is part of our duty to do the right thing, but we need to beware of becoming self-righteous. The 'self righteous' person is not the same as 'the perfect' person. We know of only one perfect person, and that is Jesus himself. We know of several who are 'on the way', following Jesus as nearly as they can, letting the Holy Spirit indwell them and keep them alert. These are the sort of people who have been of help to us and this is the sort of person we would like to be and to encourage others to be.

Questions

1. In church life many decisions are made on the basis of a demo-
    cratic vote. List the strengths and weaknesses of this principle.
    Under what circumstances may the majority be wrong rather
    than right?

2. "Self-control is mentioned many times in the scripture, yet,
    once I believe in Jesus who loves me and forgives my sins, isn't
    it possible for me to do just as I please?"

3. How far should a Christian be 'fashionable'?

4. When is it right for me to curb my impulses out of considera-
    tion for other people?

5. Is one tenth (1/10th) a reasonable proportion of one's income
    to put aside for God's work? What causes can be helped out of
    this tithe?

CHAPTER 9

Cults and Sects

One morning, responding to a knock at the door, we met two young couples who requested a supply of New Testaments to help them with their work among people in prison. This gave us an opportunity for fellowship and, as lunch was being prepared, they were invited to share our food. It was at the end of the meal, after a moment's prayer, that one of the young women declared that she loved my husband and gave him a hug and a kiss. Although my husband is not entirely averse to being hugged and kissed by members of the opposite sex, it is also clear to us both that he is no great stirrer of hearts and that anyone who felt like kissing him upon a first meeting was a little odd. This was our introduction to the Children of God, one of the cults this chapter is about.

What is a cult? Among the definitions given in our dictionary a cult is a quasi-religious organisation using devious psychological techniques to gain and control adherents or a group having an exclusive ideology and rituals centred on sacred symbols. It is also defined as something regarded as fashionable or significant. A sect, on the other hand, describes a sub-division of a larger religious group, the members of which have to some extent diverged from the rest by developing deviating beliefs. A sect can be a sub-division of any religion, Christian or otherwise.

Why do we need to know about cults? At some time or another we are almost certain to meet members of these organisations who will try to persuade us that they have a knowledge of truth that we lack and that our faith in and knowledge of Jesus Christ is not adequate for our salvation. In this chapter we will try to describe some of the cults we may meet and where their teaching goes astray.

The Children of God

The young lady who was so free with her hugs and kisses in our home demonstrates the way the Children of God think. Their reasoning is very subtle. Love, they say, is the great liberator, and you can't hate people when you love them. It is the path to release from inhibitions and from resentments; it is God-given and a path to the presence of God, for 'God is love'. While this sounds right, one soon realises that the love they are talking about is often erotic and sexy. Artists' impressions of heaven drawn in Children of God literature that we have seen convey the idea of sunlit holiday camps with trees, flowers and swimming pools, plus plenty of scantily clad females around. From the pictures it would seem that women outnumber men in heaven on an approximate 3:1 ratio!

One aspect of the cult that many find disturbing is the involvement of children. Quite often the adults who engage in door to door canvasing have one or two children tagging along with them. In Delhi we were made aware of some teenagers being lured away from their parents and home, and also that cells to contact young people can be set up near university campuses.

One means of attracting people, especially young people, into the cult is the use of music. Their musical tapes are well produced. The music is lively and the words appealing. When these tapes are sold, people are invited to make donations, implying that this will be used for the spread of the gospel.

This cult has spread into many countries, some of which have banned its activites because of its affect upon family life and young people. It tends, however, to go underground and also to change its name. In some places the group now calls itself 'The Family'.

Beware of such groups, not all of which emanate from 'the West', which promote a promiscuous sex life and emphasize the erotic. Although they may use the term 'self-sacrificing love', and even 'Agape love', they give no evidence of the love that is willing to accept discipline, self-control and suffering for the sake of the people who are the objects of such love.

The following are quotes from a little booklet of daily readings put out by the Children of God. The book is called "Daily Might" and looks at first sight rather like the little booklet 'Daily Light' which many Christians use for their daily devotions. Admittedly, these are but a few extracts from the 364 daily notes, but they illustrate how they appear to be 'Christian' but have emphases which are way out and which do not honour Christ.

Jan. 1:   It's a New Year and a new day. As we make progress, we
           have to do new things and new ways as each year goes by,
           ... If you can't think up better ways of doing it, then you're
           dead like the churches. They got in such a rut that they
           never got out of it.

Feb. 18:   Happy Birthday, Dear Family. Jesus' birth was the birth-
           day of all Christianity, but when was our special indi-
           vidual branch of the great Christian family born? Well
           the Lord showed me that it really began with me when I
           was born on Feb. 18...Let us specially rejoice in this
           day...Let's have a Happy Birthday love feast! Everybody
           kiss and hug and love everybody and tell them how much
           you love them and make up and make out.

Mar. 5:   It is not man's fault that he is born in sin. This is the fault
           of those who brought sin into the world... All mankind,
           let's face it, is sinful. But God is not angry with us for
           breaking the rules. He knows the sinner is a sinner and
           can't keep the rules... The only unpardonable sin is lack
           of faith in Jesus... He'll forgive you for every sin in the
           book except rejecting Jesus.

July 1:   Love is the most important thing in our religion. We be-
           lieve in free love! Free love of God through Jesus Christ
           His Son! We have other kinds of love, to.... True love,
           real love, is all the religion you need! This unselfish sac-
           rificial love includes the love of one human being for an-
           other, love in all its forms, as long as it is true love, real
           love, God's love. We have such sweet love in the Lord, ...
           Oh, we've got all kinds of love in our midst! Isn't it won-
           derful to have love?

Aug. 19:   If thou wilt open thy mouth to receive it, I will not only
           give thee honey and sweetness from my mouth, but I will
           give thee wine of my spirit and thou shalt tingle to the
           thrill of my ecstacies, if thou wilt receive it. Therefore
           open wide thy mouth that thou mayest receive the wine of
           my spirit and the thrills of the ecstacies of my love... If
           you can accommodate His new wine without asking why

or trying to analyse its ingredients, God has such thrills and intoxications of the Spirit in store for you, that you will be glad that you drank it without question and you will be whisked off into a world which you never dreamed existed where you will enjoy the very wonders of intimacy with God Himself in a wild orgy of the Spirit as His totally surrendered Bride.

Sept. 30: It's your floodtide... (Vision) I see a stream flowing. It takes the path of least resistance and follows and takes the lowest level. We are all being swept along with God's mainstream... God will make a way... You don't have to climb the banks or over the rocks. Try to avoid the obstructions and follow the path of least resistance, going where there is most receptivity, the most openness, always seeking the lowest level.

Oct. 25: Back to the beauty, nudity and sexual freedom of the Garden. Before Adam and Eve sinned they had pure sinless hearts and a heavenly outlook. They only became ashamed of their nudity after they fell. ... We're as free as Adam and Eve in the Garden before they sinned. ... We have perfect freedom and unpretentious liberty and unashamed fellowship and naked contact with each other, both spiritually and physically. ...

Nov. 27: We are the living church of the Living God, not whitewashed sepulchres of the dead. ... There is no law in the entire Bible that says, or even hints, that you have to go to a church building on a Sunday! ... So the true Church is not a building or a Denomination, but the genuine Christian believers... So you don't have to go to church on Sundays, you don't need church buildings or rituals...

The Jehovah's Witnesses (or The New World Society)

The JWs, as they are sometimes called, are a zealous group of people who take Isaiah 43: 10 & 11, " 'You are my witnesses,' says the Lord (Jehovah) '...apart from me there is no saviour' " as key verses. They think the end of the world is coming soon and want to save as many people as possible by baptising them as JWs. There is no salvation outside of JWs. All existing branches of the Christian Church and man-made political parties and institutions like the U.N. are in error, are Satan's agents and heading for destruction. Jehovah (or Yahweh) is the Name of Almighty God, written in Hebrew(יהוה) and basically means 'The One Who is', 'the One who is permanently and eternally in being'.

JWs began in the USA through the leadership of a man, Pastor Russell. He was followed by Judge Rutherford, Nathan H. Knorr and Frederick Franz. Russell, whose followers were sometimes called 'Russellites' took his inspiration from such verses in the Bible as the one quoted above from Isaiah and from Revelation 1:5, where Jesus Himself is referred to as the "faithful and true Witness". In this way, the basis for the JWs is found in scripture, yet it is built up into a system which plays down other truths in scripture. So we find that the process is selective and the result is lopsided. For instance, there is a tendency to set aside the revelation which God (Jehovah) makes of Himself in Jesus. They ignore the fact that when Thomas made his inspired response to Jesus as "my Lord and God" he was putting the incomprehensible fact into words. In Jesus Thomas recognised God (Jehovah). For the JWs Jesus, 'the Word' who is also identified as the Archangel Michael, is the first super-angelic being created by Jehovah. Jesus was crucified and was raised *in spirit*. From the time that Jesus was 'raised' until Pastor Russell received his ideas, God had been silent.

Pastor Russell set up 'The Association of Bible Students', which later became the International Bible Students' Association. This leads us to note that while the JWs use the Bible as a basis, it must only be understood as interpreted by the JWs. They have their own New World translation of the Bible and are only permitted to understand the Bible as explained in Watchtower Society literature and directives.

If a couple of JWs call at your house (and they usually do their missionary work in pairs) conversation may start with a question about the Bible, or with some current social crisis, but you will soon be offered some Watchtower literature. If you accept this, or if

you show interest, this will be carefully noted and you will be in for
a return visit. Bible studies in your home may be on offer, followed
by invitations to join in neighbourhood JW studies or weekly Watchtower meetings.

Other JW beliefs, rather simply stated, include among others,
that the Holy Spirit is only God's power experienced in the world.
There is no Trinity in the Godhead. Jesus, who is 'a god' returned to
earth in 1874. The Kingdom of Jehovah was delivered to Jesus at
the 'beginning of the last days' in 1914. Prophecies can be interpreted with pinpoint accuracy–which led to such dates as 1974 for
Armageddon, the great battle to be fought in a heavenly spiritual
sphere but with the result that Christ will reign on earth for a thousand years while Satan is bound. The 144,000 mentioned in Revelation 14:1-3, are the really saved persons. These are the Witnesses
par excellence and are known as The Brothers of Christ Jesus or
The Little Brothers of Christ. Those outside that number, (for JW
membership far exceeds 144,000) are known as the 'Other Sheep'.
It is assumed also that the Watchtower Society is the only organisation through which Jehovah deals with people on earth.

The JWs who, because they feel that they are the only people in
all humankind who will be saved, delight in showing themselves as
being separate from others. By conviction they do not allow blood-
transfusion, do not eat meat with blood in it, do not celebrate birth-
days, take no part in politics nor engage in service with the armed
forces.

These are certain attractions about the JWs which need noting.
These include 'No class distinction'. All JWs are 'Witnesses' and
do not recognise some as laity and others as clergy, but for administration and leadership of meetings they have chosen leaders whom
they call 'Congregational Servants', 'Watchtower Servants' etc.
They also practice voluntary service for Jehovah's work as members, called 'Pioneers'. They take good care of their own members.
They are keen to sell literature that is produced by their press. This
is a commercial project and so the sales persons may receive commission on their sales, but this is not their primary interest. However, the organisation as a whole controls millions of dollars, so

continually it has to be on guard against using power and money for
personal aggrandisement rather than for Jehovah's work, –a temptation by no means experienced only by the JWs!

The Mormons (also known as the **Latter Day Saints**).

Many sects give authority to books which they claim are of equal or
superior value to the Bible. The Mormons regard 'The Book of
Mormon' in this way. The book is supposed to be a translation of
mysterious writings in ancient hyroglyphics discovered on plates of
gold by the founder of Mormonism, Joseph Smith. He claimed to
have found these golden tablets buried on a hillside near Palmyra in
North America. Having translated the writing, the tablets were then
taken from him and returned to heaven from where they are supposed to have originally come. The name 'Mormon' comes from a
General Mormon who, it is said, lived in America around A.D. 400.
General Mormon, having written this 'record of his ancestors' gave
the plates to his son Moroni who then buried them on a hillside near
Palmyra. This same Moroni is said to be the heavenly visitor who
revealed the whereabouts of the tablets to Joseph Smith and who
later returned again to take the tablets back to heaven.

The Book of Mormon contains the record of events supposed
to have taken place between the years 600 B.C and AD 400, all on
the continent of North America. The Book of Mormon claims that
descendants of a Jewish prophet left Jerusalem around 600 B.C.
and settled in America. Jesus Christ is also said to have visited
America following His resurrection. The book contains a mixture
of the teachings that Jesus gave to His disciples and new 'teachings'
found in Mormonism.

We are often helped to sense the dubious nature of a sect by
learning something about how it came into being and who was the
founder. Joseph Smith and his family were already involved in various superstitious practices before J. Smith's claim to special revelation. They took part in semi-occult practices such as hunting for
buried treasure and water divining using a forked stick or seer-stones,
the latter were said to call on spirits to locate either the water or
treasure that was being sought. Smith is said to have been specially
gifted in these practices.

What are the teachings of Mormonism and how do they devi-
ate from accepted orthodox Christianity? Much of the Mormon teaching about God agrees with our beliefs, but they also believe that we
are all 'embryonic gods', gradually developing towards full 'god-
being'. Another aspect of their teaching about God is their belief
that He must be a tangible being with a body and physical aspects
like ours. They quote such scriptures as Jesus (Son of Man) being
"seated at the right hand of God" (Acts 7:56) as meaning that God
must have a real right hand. The verse in Deut. 4:28, comparing
idols who cannot smell, see, hear or eat, must mean that our God
has a nose with which to smell, ears with which to hear, a mouth
with which to eat and eyes with which to see!

Jesus Christ is accepted as God, but His humanity is stressed
more than His divinity. All humans are said to have had a pre-
existence in Heaven before being born through earthly parents in
the same way that Jesus existed from the beginning. They do accept
the virgin birth of Jesus, but His place as the 'only-begotten' of the
Father is somewhat blurred by the equality of pre-existence accorded
to all persons.

Mormon beliefs about the Holy Spirit are also somewhat con-
fused. They appear to accept the existence of the Holy Spirit and
the Holy Ghost as two separate spirits. One, the Holy Spirit, is the
spirit that enlightens every man regardless of his faith and is the
spirit that enables persons to know the difference between good and
evil. The Holy Ghost on the other hand, is the third person of the
Trinity and is present only with those who have been baptised and
received the laying on of hands of their priesthood. In the Mormon
teaching, baptism is regarded as essential for salvation and is given
only to thos℮ who have reached years of 'accountability before God'.
Living Mormons may be baptised in proxy for those who have died
outside the Mormon church. There are three levels of salvation that
may be attained: there is 'celestial glory' for those who have attained the highest reward and these will eventually become gods:
there is 'terrestial glory' for others who will experience the presence of God for ever but will not become gods: and a state called
'telestial glory' reserved for those who do not deny the Holy Ghost

but have not responded to the Mormon gospel. Exactly what this state will be is very vague.

Marriage has an interesting place in Mormon teaching. It is held to be essential for attaining the highest level of salvation and for this reason the early Mormons practised polygamy to give every woman the opportunity to reach heaven. In response to public outcry against this practice, it was banned from 1890 but the Mormons retain a practice of 'Celestial marriage'.

The name 'Latter Day Saints' indicates the Mormon view that we are living in the time immediately preceding the Second Advent of Christ. Their belief about the Second Coming of Christ may be summed up in words taken from their creed: 'We believe in the literal gathering of Israel and the restoration of the Ten Tribes: that Zion will be built upon this earth, and that the earth will be renewed and receive its paradisical glory'.

All who join the Mormons are expected to give at least two years to act as missionaries carrying their message to other people. It is these missionaries, who usually canvas a district in pairs, who will be found knocking at your door.

The Moonies (or Unification Church)

Most of us will have heard of the Moonies and may be will have had some contact with them. They tend to seek their converts from among young people and are often found active on university campuses or places where young tourists may be met, e.g., coach and rail termini or airports. The warmth of their welcome and their readiness to help find accommodation, etc., will be very attractive to some one feeling rather lonely and may be somewhat lost, but it is essential to be warned of the motive behind this helpfulness and the danger present in becoming involved with this sect.

Sun Myong Moon was born in N. Korea in 1920 and was a member of the Presbyterian church. From the age of 16 years Moon began to have visions in which, he claimed, Christ appeared to him and informed him that he was chosen to accomplish a great work. Moon was to fulfil the mission which Christ Himself had failed to complete. After studying in Japan during the Second World War, Moon returned to Korea and joined an extreme form of Pentecostalism. In 1945 he claimed to have had another vision in which he was told that he was to be the supreme victor in heaven and earth and that Jesus Christ bowed down to him as His superior. Moon was imprisoned and subjected to terrible torture by the Communists in his country and this left him with an extreme hatred for communism and a belief that the only way to prevent communism from overcoming all the nations of the world was to accept his, Moon's, leadership. Moon was excommunicated from the Presbyterian Church in 1948 but six years later he founded 'The Holy Spirit Association for the Unification of World Christianity', later known simply as the Unification Church whose followers accept the title of 'The Moonies'. Moon married his present wife in 1960, his previous marriage having ended because his then wife could not understand or accept her husband's new religion. The present Mr. & Mrs. Moon are the 'True Parents' called by God to establish His Perfect Family. His view of marriage and parenthood give us a clue to Moon's beliefs and also help to explain how the Moonies have gained a place in the Guiness Book of Records for the largest number of couples to be married in a single ceremony! Mass marriages between partners chosen by Moon are part of the plan to create the Perfect Family of which Mr. & Mrs. Moon are the Perfect Parents.

Let us look more closely at some of the doctrines of the Unification Church. The Bible, as we have already seen, may be superceded in the minds of members of some sects by other writings (e.g. The Book of Mormon for the Mormons, or the Watchtower publications for Jehovah's Witnesses). Moon and his followers agree that the Bible is a valuable book but say that its message may be very misleading. They say that the message of the Bible is 'coded' and that, in order to understand it, we must listen to Moon who has been sent by God to reveal its hidden message. About God and the Trinity they say, God is masculine and the Holy Ghost is feminine (an idea relating to the Eastern religious concept of yin/yang, masculine and feminine energies). Jesus Christ was sent into the world to become the True Parent of mankind. As a human father cannot bring children into being without a mother, Jesus needs the feminine Holy Spirit to bring to birth His Perfect Family. So, as we are born of the Holy Spirit, we can become true children of God. The Moonies' view on salvation and the means of salvation is totally unchristian. The first Adam, they say, was meant to be the father of the perfect human race. Eve, however, who God created to be Adam's perfect partner, sinned by being seduced by the devil and having intercourse with him. This meant that all children born to Adam and Eve thereafter were tainted by this sin of Eve. God then sent His Son Jesus Christ, the Second Adam, into the world to be the Perfect Father of the Perfect Family. But Jesus was crucified before he could find His perfect partner and therefore God's second plan was frustrated. (Note, the Cross and Crucifixion is, for the Moonies, a disaster and not God's way of salvation). According to the Moonies, God's plan now involved the sending of a Third Adam to accomplish what the first two Adams failed to do. This third Adam will succeed by achieving a perfect marriage and lay the foundation for God's Perfect Family on earth. While Moon has not himself claimed to be this Third Adam, he is widely believed among his followers to be just that, and he has done nothing to discourage this belief.

The Unification Church is also known by several other names; e.g., The Holy Spirit Association, The House Church, United Family Enterprises, The International Cultural Foundation. The Korean National Ballet which has received international acclaim, is sponsored by the Moonies and they are also involved in various commercial undertakings. The missionary arm of the church is very active and engages in a number of community based projects such as play groups for children, help for the elderly, etc. All these are very laudable occupations and attractive to idealistic young people. In their missionary work they are keen, at first, to give the impression that they are normal, zealous Christians and may deliberately set out to deceive by suggesting that they have the approval of local churches or ministers. They call this sort of thing 'heavenly deception'. People drawn into the organisation may be subjected to intense 'brain-washing' sessions often resulting in alienation from home, family and friends, examples of which have been publicised in the media.

New Age

Perhaps a few words need to be written about New Age movements. Such movements are very prevalent in Western society, especially among students and young adults, and as there is great deal of cross-culture these days, it is well to be aware of such tendencies. It is also true to say that some of the ideas found in the Western 'New Age' movement have long been known in religious systems and practices in Asia.

The title 'New Age Movements' is an umbrella term covering a variety of beliefs and practices, its adherents following only one or two trends. Such practices are not necessarily organised, so we do not find a New Age Church or Society. The practices derive from beliefs which range from Astrology to Aroma-therapy, from Crystals to Colour-therapy, from magnetism to the occult, and may include the use of mantras and meditation. Most involve a view that makes Nature or Mother-Earth into a goddess to be worshipped, and there is often an element of pantheism (all things that we see are part of God). While it is true that worthy causes such as a concern for the environment, the need to find alternative medicines that avoid creating dependency on drugs, and a sense of failure of man-made political systems to solve present-day problems, lead to a search for new answers, such a search can give rise to interest in the weird and wonderful, and allow people to make great claims for their own particular solution to problems. Most of the systems offer their followers health and happiness at no cost, no self-denial, no self-sacrificial love, no Cross! Most 'New Age' groups consist of small numbers, sometimes with a leader or guru whom they revere, sometimes forming a coven that practices a form of witchcraft. Drugs, inhalents or intoxicants may be used to induce the ecstatic experiences their believers desire, and strange rituals and language can form part of a procedure to build up an atmosphere of mystery.

It is not always easy at first to identify the danger in these practices. They may seem to be just 'good fun' or to have very real health benefits. For example, massage and the use of oils or forms of exercise are healthy. Natural herbs used as medicines being rediscovered in the West no doubt bring benefit to many. Respect and care for our much abused environment is essential, if human and animal life is to be sustained on this planet. So what is the danger? When God created this earth, He made it wholesome and good. He gave humankind dominion over it and put into it everything that is needed for our well-being. He gave us minds and intelligence to use all things well. There is no need to use mumbo-jumbo to invoke the aid of spiritual powers or to enhance the effectiveness of herbal treatments or physical exercise. Indeed, God's Word specifically decries all forms of sorcery. Glory and praise belong to God alone and, under His guidance, we can use all nature for the benefit of people. Our faith offers the benefits of creation and knowledge to all, not just to a favoured few who have been initiated by some secret rite into a group claiming exclusive access to spiritual powers.

Conclusion

We began this chapter with the story of a visit paid to our home by Children of God members. Their method of gaining our attention was to appear to have a common interest, i.e., evangelism through scripture distribution among prisoners. We have also seen in this chapter how members of cults will try to gain our interest through their social services, or through our need for friendship or dissatisfaction, perhaps with our studies, our home or even our church fellowship. Some are not averse to use of deceit or to misrepresenting themselves in order to draw us into their circle. How can we prepare ourselves to recognise and meet these often subtle attractions?

First, we need to be strong and sure in our own Christian faith. Much of what is written in this book is intended to help you do that. Knowing your Bible through systematic Bible study will help you identify errors in wrong 'Bible Teaching'. Keeping in fellowship with your church and avoiding experimenting with doubtful practices are also important. When you do have a problem, share it with someone whose experience as a Christian may be wider than yours; your pastor or Youth Leader, perhaps. It is wise to avoid getting involved in discussions or arguments with cult members. Most of them will have been well trained in presenting their propaganda and you may find yourself 'out of your depth'. If you are faced with a persistent propagandist, give a simple statement of your faith in the Lord Jesus Christ as your all-sufficient Saviour and draw the conversation to a close. In this way you will be a witness to the truth which the Holy Spirit can use. Remember the promises of Jesus, "Lo, I am with you always" and "I will send the Holy Spirit to be your counsellor and guide".

Questions

1. Are there any factors common to all cults which send out warning signals to Christians?

2. How would you react to an invitation to attend a series of meetings of the Moonies and why?

3. What do you think attracts people to join a cult?

4. Can we learn anything from the missionary zeal of many cult members?

CHAPTER 10

Stewardship

The concept of stewardship is so important in the Church that the Church of North India has a special synod-level standing committee whose job it is to see that the dioceses understand and practise stewardship. The idea covers all the practical things we do in our lives to show that we truly love God. The C.N.I. keeps the first Sunday in October as Stewardship Sunday and expects its presbyters and diocesan stewardship directors to hold an annual teaching campaign. After Bible study and preaching on stewardship, committed members of the congregation are asked to visit every home in the pastorate, to remind the families of the their duty towards God and the church, and to tell them of the programme and needs of their local congregation and diocese. As a response the members of the congregation fill up a pledge card of things they will do for the church and amounts they will give. Of course, a stewardship campaign does not take place in every pastorate or diocese but figures do show that where stewardship is taken seriously the church is self reliant in finance and personnel. A stewardship home-visiting campaign does not cover every aspect of stewardship, and some people think it lays too heavy an emphasis on fund raising. So, if we want to understand stewardship or what being a good steward means, we can look at stories about stewards in the Bible.

In the Old Testament, Joseph was the steward, first in Potiphar's household (Gen. 39:4) and then in the Pharoah's palace (Gen. 41:41). In Pharoah's regime he was put in charge of the whole country of Egypt. Joseph knew that Egypt wasn't his country and that he was not its Pharoah, but he had the trust of the Pharoah to act with authority on his behalf. He represented him in all his dealings with the people, especially in the sharing of the land's resources, and he tried to act as the Pharoah would wish. In the final analysis he was accountable to the Pharoah. When we think of ourselves as God's stewards we are acknowledging that we are not the owners of His world, or the Church or even of our special gifts. We recognise that God has created us and He is our sovereign Lord and has given us these things to look after and use for Him. We are accountable to Him as stewards.

We can find different words in the Bible beside 'steward' to express the way we relate to God. For instance, we can call ourselves 'children of God', or 'servants', but 'stewards' seems to be the best metaphor when we are talking about our responsibilities for carrying out God's will in practical matters.

In the New Testament we can see a picture of Jesus as his Father's steward with a job to do in the world in a limited time and space. As a young boy He said to his parents who were searching for Him, and eventually found Him in the Temple, "Did you not know that I must be about my Father's business?" Later He knew He was responsible for all the people He taught and in His prayer on the night He was betrayed He gave an account of his stewardship. "While I was with them, I protected them and kept them safe by that name you gave me." (John 17:12)

Jesus also taught about stewardship in several parables. In the parable of the talents in Matthew 25: 14-18, the king rewards the servants who had carried out their responsibilities well, and who had doubled the money with which they had been entrusted, with yet more responsibility. And the servant who had done nothing was thrown out as useless. The key idea behind stewardship seems to be responsibility and accountability to the Master.

In the business of human life every human being is expected to be God's steward. The earth is given to all people to use and enjoy. Christians are only just waking up to the fact that they have been some of the worst exploiters of the earth's resources, and have justified their domination of it by quoting God's injunction in Genesis 1:28, "Fill the earth and subdue it." Now, as they realise that the earth's resources are limited and have to be replenished, they are trying to be more careful. We too have to play our part in protecting the environment from exploitation and pollution. It is a really a

matter of being wise and unselfish and doing something practical in
the neighbourhood we live in. A few of us may be called to deal
with global matters like the depletion of the ozone layer, but all of
us can save water, clean the streets in our own area and plant trees.

Besides this universal stewardship of the environment, Christians have special duties. As Christians our first responsibility is to
proclaim the gospel. We are stewards of the mysteries of God, 1
Cor. 4:1. Our second special responsibility is to build up the people
of God (the Church) and maintain them by our giving and service,
Ephesians 4:12. These two responsibilities are specifically the Christian's. Besides this we are to do everything in our life as if we were
Christ's representatives. In our secular jobs just as in any church
activity we are to do it to the best of our ability and to reach out to
others, specially those in need. Whether there is a formal stewardship campaign in our pastorate or not, it is good for us to take
annual stock of ourselves and see how far we are faithful in our
stewardship responsibilities to God, the Church, our neighbours
and our environment.

As Christians in this multi-religion society we have to acknowledge that the gospel is our sacred trust. We have to be ready to
share the good news with our neighbours, telling them how Jesus
has helped us in our lives and how He is ready to help them also.
Sometimes instead of proclaiming the gospel, young people want to
hide the fact that they are Christians. We should neither be ashamed
of Christ, nor of the fact that we belong to a minority community.
Some are tempted to hide their identity because they come from a
dalit (outcaste) background and want to keep that hidden. Actually
it should be a matter of great rejoicing that the message of the gospel was taken to heart most eagerly by the poor and the oppressed
and that it has brought great joy and progress in the lives of many in
our nation. The gospel is about turning the values of the world upside down. It is about telling the poor and blind and imprisoned that
God is on their side and even willing to suffer beside them as He did
on the cross.

When we think of our stewardship of the Church, the people of
God, we have to be quite sure what we mean. Sometimes we say

"we are the chosen people of God", and we completely misunderstand what that 'doctrine of election' or chosenness means. We think it means we have been chosen as a member of the church to receive special privileges. For example, if we are not doing very well in life, we might say, "What has the Church done for me?" and we mean, "Why am I not getting a mission house to live in, or a job, or a scholarship?" Of course the Christian family should look after its own weaker members in need, but the task of the Church is to build up its people to serve the outside world in Christ's name and proclaim the gospel. The Church is Christ's 'body' trying to carry on the work that Jesus did in his lifetime. We need to be sure we understand what we are building up the Church for. We are chosen to serve.

The structure of the Church that we have to maintain has come to us in North India through missionaries and its form is heavily dependent on a western pattern. There are beautiful buildings in the centre of large towns, large plots of land, big parsonages, schools and hospitals with paid professional staff which all look impressive and as if the congregations were aiming for prestige and the running of a fine, hierarchical administration. It is all very different from the churches that were planted by St. Paul which we read about in the Acts of the Apostles, or even from the congregations that St. Thomas founded in India in the first century. As twentieth century stewards of the Church we have to be very sensible about the resources we have inherited. Sometimes it seems as if we were more interested in being chowkidars of buildings or mission compounds, than in preaching the Word of God. Again and again we must remind ourselves of our Christian stewardship and be quite sure that we invest in people rather than in buildings. The Indian Church cannot change its structure overnight, but it must develop its own ideas of what the body of Christ should look like in the Indian context and work towards that.

The church buildings that we have inherited are large and expensive to maintain, but they are our inheritance and should not be allowed to decay. (If they are really useless to us, they should be given or sold away or pulled down). As stewards we must see that they are kept in good repair and put to good use. It is a very bad witness when roofs are leaking and compounds overrun with weeds and rubbish. It may be costly to repair a church, but it would certainly be more costly to build a new one. Each of us must give his or her tithe to the church. With this money the pastor will be paid, the fabric of the church maintained and the outreach work of the church carried on. The church is financially much poorer than it need be because we people have forgotten to give willingly. Nothing reveals our love of God more than our willingness to give. Billy Graham said, "Show me your cheque book and I will tell you how much you love God." The way we spend our money proves how seriously we take our Christian stewardship.

The previous paragraph about tithing is not meant to imply that once we have set aside a tenth of our income, or time, for church work we can use the rest of our money or leisure in any irresponsible way we please. Stewardship is not so much about budgeting and apportioning time and talents as about having an attitude of being accountable to God in all things–not because He is watching out to catch us and punish us, but because we actually want to do what He wishes. We want to show Him how much we appreciate the undeserved gifts He keeps giving us. Some religions talk about 'earning merit' and their adherents want to do good so that they can earn God's favour. Christianity works the other way round. We have received God's favour without having done anything. In fact we have received His love in the midst of our sins, and so we want to do something good to show how much we appreciate this undeserved love. "We love God because He first loved us." We give to God because he first gave to us.

We have to be very sure about our Christian values when we live as a small minority in India. We cannot help but imbibe the values of our neighbours and most of them are good--like the importance of the family–but we should be able to break the rules of society if they conflict with what Jesus taught. Jesus Himself several times broke the rules of the society of his day. We should, for example, insist that a girl's worth is just as important as a boy's and rejoice at her birth. We should be clear that a person's colour or caste background or wealth does not tell us much about a person's real character or worth.

Stewardship is a serious business but it should not be dull. The Holy Spirit gives us as His first gifts "Love and Joy". These are attractive qualities and help us to plunge into life with enthusiasm.

Questions

1. What do you personally understand by Christian Stewardship?

2. In the book of Deuteronomy, chapter 6, the Jews are told to teach their children God's commandments and remind them of how He brought them out of Egypt. In that way the Jewish religion and history was handed down from one generation to another and their identity as a people formed. Do you think that the Indian Church likewise should recall for its young people its (pre-Christian) past, –or is that not important for its identity and mission?

3. What shape would you like the Christian Church to have in India in the future? (Sadhu Sundar Singh said the gospel should be offered in an "Indian vessel". What did he mean?)

www.ingramcontent.com/pod-product-compliance
Lightning Source LLC
Chambersburg PA
CBHW051930240626
47153CB00004B/1436